PRAISE FOR *JOURNEY TO T...*

'A terrific tale of love and redempt... first line.'—Nicholas Shakespear... *... ...ncer Upstairs*

'The most impressive and satisfying novel of recent years. It gave me all the kinds of pleasure a reader can hope for.' —Tim Winton

PRAISE FOR *CONDITIONS OF FAITH*

'This is an amazing book. The reader can't help but offer up a prayerful thank you: Thank you, God, that human beings still have the audacity to write like this.' —*Washington Post*

'I think we shall see few finer or richer novels this year . . . a singular achievement.'—Andrew Riemer, *Australian Book Review*

PRAISE FOR *THE ANCESTOR GAME*

'A wonderful novel of stunning intricacy, and great beauty.' —Michael Ondaatje

'Extraordinary fictional portraits of China and Australia.' —*New York Times Book Review*

PRAISE FOR *THE SITTERS*

'Elegant yet compassionate, austere yet profoundly human.' —Veronica Brady, *Australian Book Review*

'Like Patrick White, Miller uses the painter to portray the ambivalence of art and the artist.' —Simon Hughes, *The Sunday Age*

ALEX MILLER was born in London, where he spent the first fifteen years of his life. At the age of seventeen he migrated alone to Australia. His work includes *Watching the Climbers on the Mountain* (1988); *The Tivington Nott* (1989), which won the Braille Book of the Year Award; *The Ancestor Game* (1992), which won the Miles Franklin Literary Award, the Commonwealth Writers Prize and the Barbara Ramsden Award for best published book; *The Sitters* (1995), which was short-listed for the Miles Franklin Literary Award; *Conditions of Faith* (2000), which won the NSW Premier's Literary Award, the Christina Stead Prize for Fiction and was short-listed for the Miles Franklin Literary Award; *Journey to the Stone Country* (2002), which won the Miles Franklin Literary Award; and his latest novel *Prochownik's Dream* (2005). He writes full-time and lives in the Victorian country town of Castlemaine.

THE TIVINGTON NOTT

Alex Miller

ALLEN&UNWIN

My thanks are due to the poet Kris Hemensley. During the early 1980s, in his occasional magazine H/EAR, *Kris published some pieces of mine in which I referred to the Nott of Tivington. It was the enthusiastic response we received to these pieces that encouraged me to write this story.*

This edition published in 2005
First published in Australia by Penguin Books Australia in 1993
First published in the United Kingdom by Robert Hale in 1989

Allen & Unwin
83 Alexander Street
Crows Nest NSW 2065
Australia
Phone: (61 2) 8425 0100
Fax: (61 2) 9906 2218
Email: info@allenandunwin.com
Web: www.allenandunwin.com

National Library of Australia
Cataloguing-in-Publication entry:

Miller, Alex, 1936– .
   The Tivington nott.

   ISBN 1 74114 778 6.

   I. Title.

A823.3

Typeset by Midland Typesetters
Printed in Australia by McPherson's Printing Group

10 9 8 7 6 5 4 3 2 1

In loving memory of my mother and father

Alex Miller at 16 years,
West Somerset Farm,
1953

Morris, the genuine
West Country farm
labourer

AUTHOR'S NOTE

The events in this book took place in 1952, more or less in the order in which I have related them, and the characters in the story are all based on the lives of real people—I have even used some of their real names. I was myself, then, the nameless youth at the centre of this narrative—that self-conscious imposter in the photograph on the facing page. I say imposter, because a comparison of my photograph with that of a genuine West Country farm labourer—the figure of Morris in the photograph below—will reveal my pose to have been not original and my own, but a copy merely of his authentic style. My half-smile is surely an admission of my awareness of the ironic potential of my situation. I was, after all, a boy from London, who successfully posed for two years as an Exmoor labourer. But it *was* a pose and, although it was not as easy to maintain as it might seem to have been from this distance in time, that is all it was. It did not last. Eventually I became a novelist, who is another kind of poseur. As a novelist, I have been not so much a liar as a re-arranger of facts. That is the kind of writer I am. The purely imaginary has never interested me as much as the actualities of our daily lives, and it is of these that I have written. Although this story may not be autobiography in the conventional sense, it is nevertheless deeply self-revealing of its author. All the episodes, not just a few of them, may be traced back to actual events and experiences in my life, and in the lives of the people, and of some of the animals, portrayed here. There was such a stag as the Tivington nott, a horse such as Kabara, a cocky Australian who owned him, a farmer for whom I laboured for two years and who had rightly earned the nickname, 'Tiger', a labourer by the name of Morris with whom I lived, a harbourer who would know himself in the figure of Grabbe, and a huntsman of the Devon and Somerset who broke his neck while chasing a hind one winter afternoon. I loved them all, and loved the landscape they inhabited. Briefly, they were my reality.

Alex Miller
Castlemaine 2005

The doctor told Morris yesterday that he shouldn't eat so much raw pig fat. It would probably kill him before he was forty. But it is the staple diet of labouring people in this locality. Morris is not from here originally, though his wife is—her parents eke out an abandoned existence in a decaying stone cottage up behind Monksilver in a sunless cleft of the moor; a situation that gives me the creeps. Morris is a native of the open downs of Wiltshire. Boarding with him, he has become my friend. His uncle, Tiger Westall, tenants this place and Morris serves him honestly, but is his own man despite that.

Even though he is a real grinder I did not mind working for the Tiger. He is not just an uncomplicated farmer. His hard good sense about managing the farm deserts him when it comes to the matter of hunting the wild red deer on Exmoor. He fears this passion as a disability and is forever guarding himself against it. Everything he does is complicated for him by this duality in his nature. He tried to get me to address him as 'Master' when I first came here from London two years ago. It is the tradition and Morris abides by it. I respect traditions and have one or two of my own. One of them is not calling people 'Master'. I could see how much it meant to the Tiger to have me conform, however, so I did have a go at it, just to be fair. But it was no good. I couldn't look him in the eye and say it. I wasn't being stubborn. There was more to it than that.

He carries a hawthorn stick—even when he has a weighty four-gallon bucket of hot pig mash in each hand he carries this stick, jammed under his armpit. On this occasion he considered using it as a weapon—he was not accustomed to arguing with labourers. But I am a glutton for hard work and he had seen enough of that to make him hesitate before giving me a thump and firing me straight off the place. Also, there was this other complicating matter that I was not aware of then.

So, we're standing here in the yard confronting each other.

'I won't be calling you Master,' I say.

Morris is interested. But he keeps carrying forkfuls of hay across from the yard-rick to the cowshed, discreetly observing developments between me and the Tiger.

And Tiger's wife too. Watching the Master straightening out the boy, stationed in the doorway of the dairy—her kitchen. Vigilant, round and fat and all in white with tiny black eyes peering out. Keyed up. Trouble on her doorstep. Ready to make a stand over this. She's been expecting it, *looking* for it—boys from London cannot be trusted! She'd like to see the Tiger chase me off the place. My decision not to call him 'Master' is proof of what she's been saying all along.

The Tiger in front of me, hunched up and tense, red in the face and gripping his hawthorn stick. Not sure how far my rebellion might go and ready to take a swipe if necessary. 'You will treat me with respect, boy, or I shall hunt you this minute!'

Serious about it!

'I do respect you, Mr Westall. And if it suits you I will call you Boss.' My polite offer takes him by surprise. Something new to think about. For maybe five or six seconds he crouches in front of me, holding on to his reaction—considering now where an advantage might lie. Then bang! he slams his stick against the corrugated tin of the bull pen and makes me jump half out of my skin.

'Boss, eh?'

'Yes.'

He's delighted I jumped and he lets it sink in; keeping me in my place with fear. Then he brandishes his stick and turns away, heading for the dairy door and Mrs Roly-Poly; 'Get on then, boy.'

It was too easy to call it a victory. That I owed him something for dropping 'Master' was a certainty.

But what I owed him only began to emerge with Kabara the black hunter.

Last April it was, and we're on the point of a testing manoeuvre. One of my big chances to be a hero around this place. So of course I'm saying nothing. Keeping quiet. Slipping into the background and waiting for Morris to do the dirty work. He won't complain. There's a cow on heat and we're about to release the bull from his solitary confinement.

When he's not actually doing his business this two-and-a-half ton animal is secured by the neck with something like an anchor chain in a pen not much bigger than he is. Restless is not the word. He's got the insane yellow eyes of a cornered cat. A killer if ever I saw one. Eaten up with soured energy. Spending his days and nights lunging from one end of the chain to the other, smashing his scarred horns into the steel framework that confines him. He's on the look-out for vengeance!

Letting him out is like loosing a homicidal maniac for a spree. It's always touch and go. The whole enterprise teetering on the brink of injury and destruction of property. A set-up looking for damage on a large scale.

So we prepare for it solemnly.

No mucking about or high spirits. No comic conspiracies between me and Morris against the Tiger. Everything tight. That's the mood on these occasions—do the best we can then let fate take its course.

First we chain shut the gate to the main road. A sow once lifted this gate clean off its hinges and the bull would go through it without turning a hair. But we chain it shut all the same. It's a ritual with us. Getting our courage up. Pretending we're in control. Putting off the moment when Vern Diplomat V11 gets his taste of freedom.

I let the cow out from the stall into the small yard behind the milking shed and she stands there chewing, her brown eyes half closed. Then I go and open the gate through to her from the big yard, which the bull will have to cross. The Tiger meanwhile chaining the orchard gate.

Chains everywhere!

We're almost ready. Roly-Poly observing from behind the upstairs curtains. Everything quiet down here in the yard except for the smash of those big horns on the buckled frame. He's shifting from one foot to the other and letting out a bit of a moan every now and then.

We're all set.

Me and the Tiger step back a bit and look at Morris.

I've got my pitchfork. Tiger's got his stick. What a laugh! I'm supposed to guard the gate to the orchard in case the Diplomat decides to go off in that direction. Tiger will stand with his back to the dairy door, ready to bolt into the house should the bull head his way.

The bashing in the bull pen stops. We look at each other. The old boy must have caught a whiff of the proceedings. Silence for three seconds then he goes crazy, bellowing and moaning and hurling his great carcass around.

'Let him out!' the Tiger says, and he turns away, going for the dairy and safety. I look at his broad flat back and then I turn to Morris. Morris smiles and goes off to do his job. I could stick the Tiger with my pitchfork! Drive a steel prong through his tweed jacket and deep into his lung. Dig it in. See Roly-Poly come shrieking from the house. And dig her too! Something worse than her dread of all this. Be a mad bull myself. Go on a rampage! They don't care if their nephew gets pulped in that pen.

I go over and take up my position by the gate.

I'm waiting.

I'm ready to make a run for it.

The yard is empty. Morris is in there. On his own with the bull and he's stretching out on tiptoe over the horns

trying to reach the release pin on the shiny steel chain—
polished by the greases from the hide. A sudden swing of
that loaded head and Morris will be crushed. But the
Diplomat's probably sitting back hard on the chain, keeping
it stress-tight, rolling his sick eyes and choking on his
tongue, fired up to go and break that cow's back with one
almighty thrust. Too lunatic to co-operate. Just wanting to
jump her then smash everything in sight.

I'm waiting for him to come out.

And I feel certain that if I were to drive the steel tines of
this pitchfork into his eyes I wouldn't stop him. He'd just
keep coming into the pressure. Something in his nature.

I look across to where Tiger is standing by the door. It's
too far to see the expression in *his* eyes. I know it anyway.
Sullen at this point in case something goes wrong. Then
he'll go bright red in the face and start screaming abuse at
Morris. Roly-Poly backing him up. Like a couple of maniac
woodland trolls. The whole world conspiring against them.
Morris a disloyal, useless nephew who should never have
been given a job. And so on.

The moaning and choking is still going on in the pen.

I'm set to take off the minute things get out of hand. It's
a matter of personal survival. If Morris should fall under the
bull when he comes careering out that door on to the
cobbles I shan't be rushing over to distract it. I'm not living
in a land of heroes and legends.

Here he is! The huge red carcass slamming through the
door! Going too fast to know where he is, and bigger than I
remember him. He hesitates, then catches a whiff of the cow
and away he goes, ploughing his way clean across the corner

of the dung-heap, moaning and bellowing and spraying shit all over the yard. Morris after him, yelling and waving his arms, pretending to be doing the steering. But really this is all just a matter of hoping for the best. Letting nature take its course. Standing back and watching the miracle of procreation.

And he's on her! Up on his hind legs and heaves one into her. Love at first sight.

It's all over.

Now he's looking around to rip one of us apart. He swings his head and hauls a two-hundredweight chunk off the dung-pile. Spoof! he whams it into the dairy wall. Shit everywhere. Then lets out a shriek as he spots Morris heading for him with an armful of sweet golden mangolds.

If it was up to me at this stage we'd all clear out. But Morris believes in seeing things through.

There has to be a better way of doing this.

The trick now is to lure the Diplomat back into his pen by leading him along a trail of mangolds. The idea being that if we can keep him busy gutsing himself he might forget to kill us all. I can't believe he won't catch on to this strategy sooner or later.

I must endure it while he inches his way back across the yard, lifting his head every step or two between bites and spraying some saliva around, keeping us in mind of what's on for afters. Between shifts at laying the bait-trail, Morris—he's doing all this on his own as me and the Tiger are frozen to our spots—slips into the pen and hangs up the chain so that Diplomat will put his head into the noose when he goes for his final titbit, a honeyed bowl of sugarbeet!

It's really quite a nice day, if only I were free to enjoy it. The sun has come out and is warming me through my jacket. Not that I'm actually beginning to relax. I'm not doing that. But I am letting myself hope that the bull will go on doing the right thing. I can see the Tiger inching forward. Morris sees him too and waves him back. It's too soon to rejoice. I'm staying still as a rock, letting my eyes roam around, keeping tabs on the scene. Watching that big slobbering mouth stuffing itself full of sweet pulp. And the Diplomat's checking me every now and again. Making sure I'm not trying to sneak away.

It's maybe another ten yards to the bull pen when this retired Australian army officer who lives about half a mile down the road from Morris's cottage, at Gaudon Manor, Major Fred Alsop, jumps his stallion Kabara over the road gate into the yard.

I suppose he thought we'd be impressed with his horsemanship. After all, leaping from tarmac onto granite cobbles over a fixed gate at least four-foot-six high on a fiery stallion of around sixteen hands is a fairly out of the way thing to do round here in the middle of an ordinary working day. It's unexpected.

There's sparks actually flying out from the horse's shoes where they're slamming and sliding around and he's practically through the bull before he can pull up. But there's not a lot of control in it that I can see. And the horse doesn't know what he's jumped into. It's not hard to tell. He's confused and excited. Wondering what he's supposed to be doing next.

That's what we're wondering too. We're all assuming,

I suppose, that Alsop has some plan of action that he's about to carry out; and we stand there gaping, waiting for him to get on with it. The Diplomat as well. He's taken by surprise like the rest of us. Half a dripping mangold hanging out of his mouth. Staring.

And meanwhile the black horse is leaping and rearing around, threatening to pound Alsop into a stone wall any second. And the major himself only just staying up there, reefing and jerking on the reins, ripping the bit backwards and forwards as if he's riding a one-wheeler for the first time.

A spectacle! Alsop, sixty years old, wrinkled, skinny, got up in the garb of the local gentry, living out some crazy idea here in Tiger Westall's yard! All the way from the other side of the world. Paying a social call. Being a trick rider. Something! An Australian horseman in fancy dress prancing around on Exmoor. Out of a book, this bloke. A tourist!

The Tiger's the first one to wake up and he starts yelling and waving his stick. Trying to get in a jab without coming into danger. A dwarf attacking a giant! 'Get on out of my yard, you mad bastard!' Something like that. Incoherent. Okay to sell this fancy prancer hay and milled oats and one thing and another at twice the going price! Laugh at him behind his back. Dig your neighbour in the ribs when you see him turned out with the Staghounds. Terrific! But the Tiger's not going to put up with *this*. You can see that.

I'm enjoying it.

I'm hoping the Tiger might get a bit trodden under foot.

The bull takes an off-hand look around at all this capering and yelling and he tosses his head and walks straight into his pen. Going for the honeyed sugar beet without any more fuss. Morris is in after him in a flash and has him chained up again.

Alsop's off the horse by now and he and the Tiger are working something out. A bit of heat from Tiger, but after all, this man's got money to spend and there's no real harm done. I'm ordered over to hang on to the horse while they go into the house for a drink and a chat to settle it all up. Alsop greets me by my first name but I pretend I don't hear him. I'm glad to see the back of him. Tiger'll fix him up. And that'll cost him a pound or two one way and another. Still, he's ripe for it. He'd be over at the cottage attending Morris's card nights, this bloke, if Morris weren't a bit too cagey for him. He's a dreamer. That's clear.

Morris comes to the door of the bull pen and stands in the sunlight and rolls a smoke. His back to the Diplomat. Everything under control. Taking his time. Getting his reward now. Idling. Enjoying the moment of leisure while he attends to the details of his own pleasure. He doesn't look across at me. Not on this occasion. He's no help when it comes to horses. He's not interested in this impressive entire that I'm hanging onto. Tractors. Motor cars. He knows all about them. Machinery. That's his idea of what it's all about. Given half a day off he'll follow the hunt from the front seat of his motor car with a pair of binoculars. That's the way to do it, according to Morris. Stay dry and comfortable. Never far from a thermos of tea, and if things don't work out you can head home without any fuss and bother. That's the way he goes hunting. His wife beside him. They're very close those two. There's a lot I don't know about them. It's another world. And they keep it closed. But horses are his blind spot. And this animal of Alsop's doesn't impress him. He doesn't want to know about it. Anyone else would come over and start theorising about breeding and condition and schooling and all that stuff. But not Morris, he wanders away after a minute, down to the orchard to take a look around.

I'm left here holding the stallion on my own. Like Diplomat, I can see there's no fear in this animal. Energy! Lots of energy. And maybe a touch of insanity too. But no fear. He's shivering, a continuous tremor running over the surface of his skin. Prepared for anything. Ready to go. So I decide to walk around with him. Something to do. Show him the place.

He can kill me if he wants to. The decision is his. He's a big energy-packed aristocrat stepping alongside me. Keeping the reins loose. Not hanging back and waiting to be led, not waiting to be told what to do. None of that. Not plodding along behind me but right here next to me. Head up and alert. Intelligent. He's not going to miss anything. Wanting to check it all out. Wanting to know where he is and what it all amounts to. He has a curiosity in him that alerts me too. A matter of paying attention. Keeping my mind focused.

We go along, from one end of the yard to the other. He stares into the bull pen, nostrils working, eyes seeking it all out in the half-light of the interior where the massive bulk of Diplomat is imprisoned.

Shoulder muscles just brushing against me as he breathes.

Let's move on!

His decision.

What's over there? I go along with him and he hurries me, energy flowing through him, moving me faster than I want to go comfortably, making me keep on my toes. Then he stands and stares at the cow. She's chewing again. Her back still arched. Big brown eyes dull and dreamy. Set for eternity! Kabara lets out a tight, aggressive grunt and moves away sharply, almost wrong-footing me, his head going down without warning; snuffling the cobbles, grunting and blowing.

We complete the circuit and stand in the middle of the yard. Surveying the scene. Has he missed anything? He is still. His hard-muscled shoulder leaning against me. And it begins to seem to me that he doesn't mind being with me. I can feel it. The way he's looking out and away from the two of us. And not peering down sideways at me, suspicious of what my intention might be. I try returning the pressure of his shoulder, wondering how conscious he might be of my touch. I'm not pushing at him, just holding a pound or two firmer. He's a sire! Words like noble, beautiful, heroic, they're making sense. I'm beginning to see what all the fuss is about.

It's something new to me.

Tiger's two chestnut hunters don't have it. They are just horses. Nobility doesn't come into it with them. H for horse. That's about it with Tiger's geldings. I should know. No comparison to this thing of Alsop's. May as well be another species. Horseradish.

It's looking after Tiger's hunters that's my special job. My particular area of responsibility you might say. The horses belong to me the way the machines belong to Morris. And the Tiger tutors me himself. It's not all fun and games. Clipping, shoeing, grooming, feeding, exercising, cleaning out, polishing the gear, worming, whatever. You name it. He likes to turn out just right on hunting days. He doesn't want anything left to chance. Hunting is his reward in life for all the skimping and grinding. Hunting the wild red deer. They've been doing it here since the Anglo-Saxon kings were around. It's not something they just decided on yesterday. It's in their blood. And the Westalls have been here forever, so when it comes to his hunters the Tiger watches me every inch of the way. Criticising mostly. Offering abuse. Sarcasm. Looking for perfection where it isn't to be found. If he says nothing I know I'm doing extra well.

I do the best I can. But perfection is not something you can get from those geldings.

Kabara, I'm deciding, is another story. I can feel the quality of this beast standing next to me. It's got something to do with ancestry. Breeding. Lineage. Stuff like that. Oats and polishing and clipping and grooming won't fake it.

The horse and I make the decision together and walk over to the gate. We stand staring down the road. Just looking. I have read in an old book on venery that men are better when riding, more just and more understanding, and more alert and more at ease . . . The sun is warm on my back and the day is calm. Going on towards noon now, and everything quiet down the road.

But that was last April when, despite the warmth of the day, there were still packed scallops of dirty snowdrift left out in the sunless hollows of Codsend Moor and Dunkery Hill. Remnants of the vicious winter that had gone before. And the strange sight of the new shoots of the deer sedge and the dark green cotton-grass poking up through flutes of melted ice, where the peat bogs had frozen to a depth of eight inches and more during the February blizzard.

Alsop and Kabara both a world away then from where they are now.

Alsop and his wife got smashed up coming back from Taunton at high speed one night in July. Midsummer and living it up. Carefree! Driving like a young man and the T junction at Handycross slipping his mind. So they hit a four-hundred-year-old wall. Which wouldn't have happened to a local. No matter how carefree. A reflex swing of the wheel at that point and a local would have gone past laughing. One of the dangers of being an alien. A local's always got something extra on you. They can feel the shape of the country in their bones. And they can afford to wait for outsiders to make a mistake. Saying nothing. Being there and waiting. Like the wall. Six foot thick. A remnant from a sturdy past and Alsop speeding along with his foot held confidently on the throttle as if he were still in the emptiness of Australia.

She's probably going to keep going till she's a hundred, but he's finished. You've only got to look at him. Getting out of the house is just him proving to everyone that he can still walk. Grey and struggling. Whatever it was that got smashed inside him, it will never come right again. He's not certain whether he can still hope for something or not. No confidence about anything now. It's downhill all the way for him from here. Staggers and slogs his way across the fields, struggling against the wind, and stands there panting, watching me and Morris getting a putt-load of mangolds out of the clamp. You get the feeling he's about to hop in and start helping you. Then he'll see we're not breaking our rhythm and he'll pass some remark. A comment he's made up. Nothing much. And away he goes. Dragging himself back the way he came. Pausing on the horizon to wave his stick and look down on us. Morris has been kind to him from time to time and I suppose that's it.

He came to the stables a couple of times and stood looking at Kabara. Nothing to say on those occasions. There's always been something about him that was totally out of step with this place. That couldn't be accounted for simply because he was a foreigner. Something that led him from time to time into being ridiculous. He turned up at his first meet of the Staghounds wearing hunting pink. Everyone, except him, knew this was something reserved for the Huntsman and the whips, but no one said a word to him about it. They exchanged glances, not smiling, not passing judgements, and they looked at each other again the same way when they heard he'd hit the wall at Handycross.

I could have told him. You've got to keep your head down in a place like this. Take it all a step at a time. Wary! Charging around in red coats and leaping bang into the middle of them on black stallions is not the way! Provide yourself with back-up and keep something in reserve! Let *them* do some of the guessing.

His wife came over to see the Tiger a couple of days after the smash. A few scratches and a bruise here and there, but apart from that you can see she's going to live forever. One of that sort. Hardy. And a touch of luck about her. The kind that walks away from a bomb blast with all her clothes blown off but herself still intact. A cigarette stuck in her mouth all the time and messy-looking. Wearing an old black dress and gum boots. Not the peacock of the family in other words. And swearing a lot. Which has the Tiger on edge at once.

She wants someone to look after the stallion till things get back on an even keel. Can the Tiger assist? She's practical. Matter-of-fact. Straight to the point almost before she's through the front gate. No hedging around with, It's a nice day, or, How are you? Just, Let's go! Let's pick up the pieces and get things rolling again! That's her attitude. You can see the way she operates. Not in mourning for any lost dream. Expecting everyone to drop what they're doing and to start listening to her. Every now and then there's a hint of an English accent in her voice that makes you wonder. And she has an aggressive way of looking at you suddenly, when she's not actually talking directly to you. Challenging. As if she almost expects you to be on the point of disputing what she's saying. I get the feeling she could come down pretty hard on someone she decided not to like.

The Tiger comes to some financial arrangement and I'm sent off with her to do what I can with the horse. Even though it's only going to be extra work for me, what with haymaking under way and everything else going full pelt in the middle of July, I still consider this a windfall. I'm looking forward to seeing something of Kabara on a regular basis. And anyway, the days are long.

The house is a big red-brick place with stone windows and timbering. Not a real manor house. A replica in a few acres of park, with a terrace looking across the valley towards the Quantock Hills. High clipped beech hedges and a gravel path raked clear of weeds and rubbish. All spick and span.

She bends down and snatches at fallen twigs as we go along towards the stables. These are off to one side, through an arch in a brick wall which is connected to the kitchen end of the establishment. There's a sandpit and first-class accommodation for four hunters with a tack room and feed store. Through a gate in the adjoining hedge I see an extensive vegetable garden, laid out in rows, and several hothouses.

She's watching me taking it all in.

And I realise it's her. She's the worker round here. Not a minute to lose.

She doesn't go near Kabara. He's checking us out from his stall. She points in his direction and says, 'I suppose you must know what to do or he wouldn't have sent you would he?' I get the impression she'd be happy to see the back of the horse. 'Give us a yell when you want a cup of tea,' she says and heads for the house.

The horse is no trouble to me. As the weeks go by I realise it's a decision he's made. I'm no Irishman to work magic with horses. It's him. He has decided I'm okay. And pretty soon the Tiger starts showing more than an idle interest. The ease with which I get along with Kabara intrigues him. But he keeps his distance. Leaving it all to me. Not making his interest too plain; watching to see how things work out. Making no move to get to know Kabara. Nothing like that. Staying a stranger to the horse. And that's his mistake.

I'm watching the Tiger too. Keeping abreast of his little schemes as they're running through his head. I have to. And I don't think he understands that this horse is not really the good-natured nag he seems, but is a potential stroke of lightning. Looking back it is easy to see how Tiger makes this mistake. He sees me crawling all over Kabara without any caution and jogging along the Wiveliscombe road with a loose rein and no saddle.

But *I* never forget for a minute the energy of this entire, and his potential for something like heroic action. You can't touch him without knowing it, no matter what you might imagine from a distance.

It's in his blood.

A feeling that he's preparing for something.

A big day when it's all going to come together for him. When all the lineage, and all the breeding and all the care and all the years and the generations of refining are going to be called finally into action. He has a performance in him, and being close to him I feel it. But it's held in reserve and would have to be *called* out of him at the big moment. His rider would have to be his equal in potential or the limit would not be reached. That's the way he makes me feel. He's ordered, disciplined, quietly under control. Waiting. For the day. This is the only way it makes sense. My 'good' reflexes are a joke in comparison with his. Kabara can react and restore his balance in the instant before I have had time to register what is going on. So I don't kid myself. I'm just taking care of him. He's out of my class. Out of Alsop's too. Out of most people's. Needing someone as special as himself to call out that performance. So I don't try anything fancy with him. I let him know what's going on, but I let him lead.

I say nothing to anyone about all this. And between haymaking and everything else, whenever we get the odd chance, which turns out to be mostly around late evening, me and Kabara are left alone to get on with things for a while. The Tiger keeps his eye on us and slips the odd question about the horse, but I don't say too much and I can see he's seriously starting to entertain the idea of hunting on him one day himself. Maybe it's no more than an outlandish fantasy at this stage rather than an actual idea. But the germ of it's there sure enough.

This horse is not an Exmoor hunter. Without superior horsemanship he's the wrong horse for this place. The first time I take him out on the Chains he panics when his feet start sinking into the bog. The local ponies skip their way over such places. Kabara thinks the earth is opening under him. And when I show it to him again, dismounting and leading him forward, giving him a good look, he makes it clear we aren't going that way. Ever!

It was about then that I decided to let him take over. Thundering along on the sound heather of the table-lands suited him just fine. But getting among the bogs and drainage ditches and old broken bits and pieces of sheep fencing, the worst of which was downed wire hidden among the bracken, was not something that interested him at all.

And it wasn't courage he lacked.

He had too much sense. Too much instinct for himself and for his own preservation. I could point him down the steepest combe and it wouldn't worry him. He'd pick his way without fear. Alert to every danger. Then one day, when there was a brief lull before the beginning of the harvest, I took him out early. Had him ready and saddled up in the yard before daylight so we could get away straight after milking, taking my breakfast with me and heading for the remote streams at the headwaters of the Barle. Taking Kabara to visit the lonely spot where I had discovered the soiling pit of the Tivington nott.

By midday we were there. Out on the tops. Then down through the steep larch woods rising up on either side of us and at the bottom a black and peaty wallow. The air rich with the stench of wet earth and rotting vegetation.

Private here. Unvisited. The depth of the wood, where the great stag-without-horns rolls and soils, cooling his body in the black mud, away from any eyes but those of the wilderness.

As we step forward, entering the dim glade, there's a whiff of mint hanging in the still air. He has moved out silently ahead of us, crushing the wild herb that grows on the edge of the stream as he stepped away. I can see his slot there, the brown mud still circulating slowly where it has filled with water. And a tiny whirlpool where his dew claws have shifted a pebble.

Kabara's senses are stretched to the limit here. Picking up the smell of the male deer close by. A slight tremor of expectancy running through his withers, transferring his readiness to me. There is a balance now in the horse, as if his hooves are not quite touching the ground, an alertness that almost tempts me to action. To leap miraculously into the dark forest after the deer . . .

I keep still.

Watching.

But we are not going to see the nott. He is in the shadows, watching *us* I dare say. I examine each dark patch of shade with care, letting my gaze rest for a moment on every uncertain shape amongst the gloomy conifers. But I can't tell where he might be. A knowing survivor. Somewhere between sixteen and twenty years old, Morris has told me. Surviving now by infinite skill and care. Old for a red stag. He's eluded the hunt on numerous occasions. Tricked them. And created a legend for himself. Many consider him dead. And none of them know he has moved to these woods or they'd come after him again. It is their practice always to take a nott stag whenever one presents himself, for they fear that notts will breed and diminish the elegance of the species.

I'm not about to tell them where he is.

Tell them nothing. *They're* the locals. And he's a long way from Tivington now. They chased him once too often and he shifted his ground right out of the district, crossing the Beacon and the Quarme and the Exe and setting himself up way over here.

I discovered him by chance and swore Morris to secrecy. Being from Wiltshire makes the secret easier for him to keep. A local couldn't hang onto such a hot piece of information for long. To harbour a stag for the hunt is the ambition of every yokel in this neck of the woods. And keeping the whereabouts of the Tivington nott a secret would burn a hole in their brains. Simple as that. You couldn't trust them with it.

The Tiger would give money to know it!

They'll find him anyway. One day. Of their own accord. And when they do he'll be on the run again. Sooner or later, when the Arctic weather is tightening his belly, he'll sneak into someone's turnip field. And then some half-witted labourer, arriving to shift the hurdles, will see his great slot there, superimposed on the sheep tracks of the day before and frozen into the mud in the morning. The footprint of the devil staring him in the face!

The yokel will drop everything and run to tell his master. Crazy to see those big hounds having a go. Howling and wailing and crying on the trail! Lighting everybody up with his news that there's a warrantable stag harbouring in the area.

Except you don't need a warrant to hunt a nott. It's open season on them all year round.

Solitary. Always on guard. Never at ease with the herd.

It was late one October afternoon a year ago that I found him. I'm following this stream to its source. Just for the pleasures of exploration and of being on my own. It's Bampton Fair day and the Tiger's been forced by one of his own traditions to give us most of the day off. He'd squirm out of it if he could, but Morris doesn't ask on these occasions. The local custom is good enough for him. He makes sure the Tiger knows what his plans are in good time, and he and his wife go visiting her parents, over to Monksilver for the day.

Too bad for the Tiger!

I get out as fast as I can too. As soon as the milking's done I'm gone. It's either that or get trapped by Tiger into doing some five-minute job that ends up taking all day.

I get away!

Right out of the place. Gone. Saying nothing. On my own. Heading off by a roundabout route till I'm way out on the moor. Keeping always to cover. Making the most of my opportunity for penetrating the wilderness.

Soon I've got my head down and I'm moving along quietly. Up the twisting track of the steep combe. Going deeper into the woods. Following the stream-bed and checking the small things. On the lookout for the unusual. Letting nothing pass. Turning the stones in the water. Sniffing at the weeds and herbs and seeking among the dense variety to get to a knowledge of it. It absorbs me. I never know what I am going to come across next. Human beings have been moving through this land for thousands of years. Leaving this and that behind. Not much, but something, every now and then, a thing out of place among the leaves and water-worn pebbles because of shape or texture. No more than a stone itself maybe. Odd man out. Giving you the sense it has been brought. And the flow of the stream is always uncovering new layers.

Crawling, when I have to, through the tough undergrowth, and wading when there's no other way. Squirming and pushing and scrabbling my way right into the silent coverts that no one visits. To see what's there. And I sit without moving under the ripe canopy of thorn and bramble. Staring. Hardly breathing. Feeling it all close and intense around me. Waiting for me to move on so that it can return to action. And rising in me the feeling that I want to break my alien fears against its wary inhabitants. Surprise them. Hunt them.

And that feeling keeps me there for a while.

Then I go on. Moving away from it. Returning to the enjoyment of the day. And I don't notice that I'm entering the mouth of a hidden glade under the dark canopy of the larches, and the stream-bank on either side a bed of needles. Soft and deep. Undisturbed.

Until the nott barks a sudden warning. I stop dead in my tracks. My heart thumping. I don't know what it is and can see nothing at first.

Then, stationary in the dark jumble of shadows, I see him. The wide-set, slanting eyes of a satyr. Wild and aggressive. Staring directly into mine. Neither of us moving. His thick neck-hair shaggy and standing out, knotted and sopping, with black mud cascading from his flanks. Something mad and savage rising from the wallow to confront me!

Staring at him it takes me seconds to work out that I am looking at a red stag and not at something from rumour and fear.

Alone in the woods with an escaped maniac!

Running won't get me far. One swift stride and he'd be on me. It's October and the rut is in full swing. And although I've heard often enough that stags will not attack humans, even during the rut, I feel sure this sudden confrontation will prove the exception to that.

Dripping with muck, caught unexpectedly in his most private moment, the breath steaming from his wide nostrils, surrounded by the rich peaty stench of his pit and the acid aroma of his heated body. This animal does not look afraid of me.

Despite his lack of antlers there is no mistaking him for a hind. His stink is of maleness and there is in his gaze that obsessed look of arousal that is not something to be argued with. The general belief is that notts do not achieve breeding rights over their antlered brothers during the rut, but with the belief is a superstitious fear of the exception. I have never seen a nott before this day, but this one is unmistakable. He is something different. An aberration even among such outcasts. I can see that. Who knows what he might do? He looks to me to be capable of anything. Any sudden extreme.

I'm not hanging around to find out.

I ease my weight onto my toes and very slowly, taking extreme care to make no sudden movement, I make ready to start backing off. The instant I tense up he barks again. I freeze. It is a sharp, urgent warning. A mad shout in the forest! And a wave of fear goes through me. As if in slow-motion I see him gathering himself. Then he leaps away to one side and is gone.

I take hold of a branch, steadying myself, listening . . .

The woods are silent again and still. Only his smell remains. As if I have imagined him but for that and for the fact that my heart is racing. I stand there for some minutes. Uncertain whether to go at once or stay. Cautiously, then, I approach his soiling pit. An intruder now in this glade. I look down at the watery slurry of the pit where he was cooling himself a moment ago. It is in a depression to one side of the stream and hidden by a stand of bracken that has asserted itself despite the larches. It is a soak. A source that perhaps becomes a running spring in wet years. Though these sources seem to stay the same whether the years are wet or dry. All around me is the intimate evidence of the old stag's activities . . . He was here before the bear and the boar and was hunted by the wolf since the beginning of his line. And he is here still. The wild red deer has survived them all.

Preserved for pleasure.

Standing here in the intense quiet I get the feeling I am being watched. I look around. Stare into the deepening shadows of the wood. Nothing moves. There's not the sound of a bird or the least rustle of a branch. No breeze. The late afternoon air of the high combe is growing cold. I hold my breath, straining my hearing, staring hard at the grey lichened trunks of the larches around me—thousand-year-old granite pillars!

Nothing!

Only there, faintly, in the extreme distance and barely penetrating this deep wooded cleft in the hills, the sound of a clocktower bell from a village somewhere. That's all.

I head, for home.

Striking down the stream at a good pace. And then from behind me there comes the sudden roaring challenge of an old stag assured and firm in his rut. The whole darkening combe around me filling and echoing with his deep bellowing, low, archaic and malicious towards men and hounds and horses, tailing off into a bolking and rattling in his throat.

The Tiger smokes du Maurier cork tips. Out of a tin. The first time I saw his fat fingers groping around trying to get the silver paper unwrapped I laughed. I thought someone must have given him the fancy cigarettes as a present. A joke. They reminded me of people in the West End. But they are his regular smoke.

An affectation.

It shouldn't have surprised me then, that he had dreams for himself. Looking back I see that things started to develop when we had our minds fixed on the harvest.

It's the end of August and we're carrying the last field. Barley. Seventeen acres called Solomon's. On the point of achieving a record crop for the Tiger. Plenty of his cronies in the same boat. Those, like him, who miss the big storm the day before the Winsford meet. Those who don't get their corn driven into the ground.

We're building the rick bang in the middle of the hot sun. Not a patch of shade in sight. And I'm slapping the sheaves down on to the grappling rattling non-stop elevator tines as fast as I can. Faster! My arms are aching so much I feel like crying. The tendons most of all, inside my elbow. Scorching with pain. I want to crawl away somewhere cool and have a good old bawl all on my own. Roll around in agony and get it out of my system. But I can't slow up.

It's the boys from the village! There's two of them up there above me on top of the load pushing the stuff down. Bombing me with it. The sheaves are rolling and tumbling down on me so fast if I stop I'll be buried. I'm lifting a pair of sheaves on to the elevator and there's more pounding right on to the end of my pitchfork. They're aiming them. Catching my arms tensed and lifting. Wham! The pain shoots right into my shoulder. But I've got to do it.

It's no good yelling out.

No one's going to slow up.

It's a race. And the Tiger's showing me who's master and who's boy. He put them up there. We've all gone mad. And he loves it. I'm choking half to death in the dust and the heat and the flying straw. And the sheaves are coming down thick and fast. Straw and chaff and needles of dried thistle going down my neck and up my nose. I don't even have time to think about when it might end. I'm too busy saving myself from being engulfed.

And the Tiger's haring around here and there and everywhere with a huge shiny grease gun held out in front of him. He's squirting and pumping and pushing the thick black stuff into every bursting nipple on the machinery till there's grease popping and dripping out all over in the hot sun. He's making sure this lunatic circus keeps going at red-hot top speed. Not going to lose a minute anywhere along the line. A mad grinder at full stretch!

As I heave the sheaves up on to the snatching steel claws, jammed into my airless pocket between the load and the roaring elevator, I catch a glimpse through the whirling haze of Morris's face poking out of the pitch hole. He's up there in the oven under the tin roof of the Dutch barn. Jammed up there by the rising rick. Right at the top where the elevator's spewing its never-ending train load into the hot, dark cavity. He's the builder. The skilled man. At the point of delivery. Putting the whole act together so it won't sag or bulge or sink down or pop out before we get around to threshing it. It's no fun being up there but no one's going to be relieving him. It's his responsibility. Tiger's making sure of that. Morris is always the one. That's what he's been doing every day for the past three weeks.

No rain. Not a storm. Nothing. Not even a burned-out bearing or a busted gasket to hold up this harvesting streak that's driving these farmers out of their heads with excitement. It's been all their way. First it was the horse beans, then the wheat, then the oats, and now it's the barley. We've all been at it. But Morris has got the killer job. The really bad one. I don't even like to think about it. I've got my own problems.

I keep going.

And his face pokes out every now and then. He's sucking fresh air and fighting off exhaustion. I slap the sheaves on as fast as I can. I'm praying he keeps that hole clear. I'm praying he doesn't let a big snarl of sheaves get rolling and bouncing at the top, tumbling down and pushing everything aside. Creating a foul-up for me to clear. I'll go under. I'll collapse. I'll come to a gasping standstill if that happens.

I'm down here in my own hole clawing at this mass of stuff and groaning aloud. Those boys are going to bury me if they can. They're going to force me to bring this show to a standstill. They're not going to be reasonable about it. They'll keep the pressure right on me. Hard as they can. And the worse it is for me the more they're going to enjoy it.

The Tiger's tucked me in nicely this time!

There's nothing I can do about it. Keep going. That's all. They're up there getting their revenge. Punishing me for staying out of their way. For being anti-social. Thinking I'm too good for them. For not going along and laughing at their jokes down the back of the bus when they go looking for a bit of tit in Taunton on Saturday evening. For being an alien. A foreigner.

They're going to send me back to London in a box if they can.

Six o'clock this morning when Tiger started the motor. Now what time is it? Who knows? I feel as though I've been going for fifteen hours. More! I can still see those aisles of stooked barley stretching to the horizon. Solomon's must have grown to ten times its normal size since this morning— and since the other day, when ancient Sam Jones and his silent white-haired brother Bill came up from the village and scythed the headland swathe under the Tiger's anxious scrutiny. Before putting the binder in. Then it looked innocent enough. Just another field of barley. No threat to anyone. The last of the harvest. I had the feeling then that it was almost over. Nearly time to calm down. Just Tiger and his superstitious obsessions. Getting the old men to put the scythes in first. Avoiding mischance. Accidents that are always sudden and strange. In the middle of work. Having no explanation. Everyone shocked and looking on. The Tiger insuring himself against the possibility of ill-luck smashing him aside just when he's got his mind fixed on big profits. Money! Taking no risks. Playing it inch by inch according to the rules that no one talks about. The rules they all think really matter most. Everyone solemn and waiting. Watching the Joneses whet their blades and no discussion now, at this late stage, about what the stand might yield. Nothing of that till it's in the rick. Safe under the tin and out of the way. And those two old wrinklies from a hundred years of smoking hearths bowing and scraping and calling him Master and touching their caps. Leading him around by the nose! They've got him. Their, say-nothing-look-knowing attitude. That's got him. He can't go against it. He's sure his machinery will fall apart in a rusting heap if he tries anything clever like that. Otherwise he *would* ignore them. And they know it. But he's seen it happen. Seen a few smart alecs spewed aside. So he's holding on. It's only the profit that he cares about. And he's going to do whatever he has to in order to get it. On the statement from the bank. That's where he wants it before he gets cocky. Then watch him go!

The little Ferguson drags its empty cart away and for a second there's a drift of clean air washing over me before the Nuffield roars in hauling its eight tons behind it! It really scares me, this one. Towering over me and blocking off the air. And he's too close in! He's pulling it too close to the elevator feed tray this time! I can see it happening. He's supposed to pull in on the old tracks. Here he is sneaking over another foot. I'm not going to have room to move!

I scream out for him to back off!

But it's too late!

The big orange diesel practically brushes my shoulder going past and the sheaves are raining down before the load stops swaying. There's nothing I can do about it. I rip into the falling sheaves. The stench from the exhaust of the elevator motor is knocking me out. It's rich and heady, taking the lining clean off the back of my throat. Those yokels are up there. Way over my head. Breathing clean air. And they're grinning at each other. It's a massacre. They're going to exterminate me if they can. They're making the most of their last

31

big chance. They must have clued the driver up and now they're not going to hold back on this one.

I'm getting a beating!

I'm trapped in here and the handle of my pitchfork's snagging on the side of the load. No room to turn. My hip bumping the polished, vibrating steel of the feed tray as I try to swivel around to pick up sheaves. I've been guarding this fork with my life for the past three weeks. Taking it home with me at night so no one would grab it ahead of me in the mornings. It's just right for this job normally. Short and sturdy. But now even it is too long. Awkward. Dangerous. It's what accidents are made of. I know. I can feel it all happening around me. I'm not in control. I'm in a hell-hole. Stuck at the bottom of a shaft, surrounded by screaming high-speed machinery, dust, prickles, fumes and falling barley!

I'll yell out! I'll plead with the Tiger for a bit of relief. The minute I see him coming round with his grease gun I'll scream out, 'Hey, Master!' That should do it. That ought to stop him in his tracks. Pull him up with a jolt. That should be worth some rest. Maybe he'll even let me drive the Ferguson for an hour or two. Get out there in the field with the loaders and the clean air. Driving along the aisles looking over my shoulder. Watching the yokels work! Run over one of them. Crush one. Pin him down under the fat tyres and watch him staring up at me. Gasping for air! Make him an item in next week's *Free Press*: YOKEL SQUASHED ON EXMOOR FARM!

But where's the Tiger? I don't see him coming round and the sheaves are pelting down thicker and faster than ever. Thump! Wallop! Here they come! Two, three, four at a time! An avalanche! They're burying me. My feet are pinned by the rising mass. I can't move. I'm stuck fast in the pile-up and they're still pushing them down on me. I can't keep my balance. I'm tilting towards the feed tray. Going into it. I'm going over. More sheaves pounding right on to me. Suffocating me. I scream out. No one can hear. I'm going over. Being overwhelmed by rural England!

Suddenly the barrage stops. And here comes the Tiger yelling at me to clear the elevator and switch off the motor.

'Yes, Boss.'

It's midday.

And there they all go. Heading for the food and drink on the other side of the rick in the shade. I pile on the sheaves. Clearing the knotted heap from around my feet. Emerging. I slap the last one on and watch it riding up on the claws of the elevator. I've got my finger on the button and the moment it clears the pitch hole I short-circuit the motor. Everything rattles to a standstill and Morris peers out the hole. He's done for and praying there's a breakdown at last. He doesn't dare hope it's really midday. But I give him the thumbs up and he grins with relief.

I'm drenched with sweat. I don't want to move. The soaked crotch of my breeches is filled with chaff and thistle debris and has rubbed me raw. I'm all pain. It's washing over my body in waves. Waves of hot blood. And I stand here with my eyes closed. I'm rocking along. Buzzing and humming and vibrating. A jangling bundle of dancing nerves. I'm getting off a merry-go-round after six hours of non-stop spinning, and I've got to get myself together into one whole piece before I move or I might fall over.

I'm standing here letting my arms hang by my sides. My body won't be ready to go again in one hour. Suddenly this Australian voice breaks in on my thoughts. Clear and close to me in the quiet drift of settling dust. 'The missus tells us you've been doing a good job with my horse. Would that be right?'

Alsop's standing at the corner of the rick. He's cool and clean. Pale blue shirt with pockets and white cotton trousers. With some kind of Spanish espadrilles on his feet. No socks. It's the first I've seen of him since his accident. He looks older. An old man now. Thin, and crouched. As if someone's just kicked him hard in the stomach and he's trying to pretend it doesn't really hurt. He's putting a lot of his weight on a stick and he's staring hard at me. Tense. Not really being friendly.

'She reckons you're a bit of a wiz with the horses.'

I suppose I'm just staring at him. He's after something. I sense it at once. The way he's come up on me suddenly like this. And now pushing and anxious. As if he's worried he might get the wrong reaction out of me or something. I don't know what's going on.

'Well good on you,' he says. Picking up on my mistrust and trying to sound at ease. 'You must have it in you. That horse was never easily managed.'

Who cares what he thinks? I don't want to talk to him. I've had it, and anyway it's obvious he wouldn't like the idea of me and Kabara getting along. He's supposed to be the magic man with horses. The *horseman*! Not me. That's his claim to fame round here, if he has one. Or was. And he might have believed it, though no one else ever did. And not much hope of going on with that now, by the look of him. He's not recovered. Despite the bright new summer outfit. He's just up and about. And *only* just. Teetering, if anything, on the brink of being entirely feeble. Even this eddying luminous air charged with barley particles still whirling round the rick is making him gasp.

He's moving towards me. I bend down and give the motor a quick wipe, avoiding his stare. 'I've just been looking after him,' I say, keeping my chin down on my chest and starting to clear out. I'm getting away from him. Going for some drink and food. Putting the elevator between us. Let him talk to the Tiger if he wants conversation. I'm too whacked to care about him. He's a nuisance. And anyway, what's he up to? He's not being straight. And that's his trouble here. He's playing at life. Playing at being a retired gentleman. And now he's getting some other thing going. I don't want to know what it is. Nothing in it for me. That much is certain. It's hard enough round here for me keeping myself intact without working out some mystery with a foreigner. I can do without his attention.

But he's following me round the rick. And I can see the two yokels down there coming round behind him. Looking for *me* and getting a bonus. Mimicking his frailty. They're munching already on hot home-baked pasties, clutching spares, and swinging a bottle of cider around. Brushing up against each other and giggling. Looking for a bit more fun at my expense.

As I come round the corner of the rick Morris looks up at me and jabs his thumb down at the space he's saving alongside him. I get over there as fast as I can. Safety. Barley!

I'm in! He nudges me with his knee and gives me a really good smile. I close my eyes and rest my back against the solid wall of the rick. Built by a good man. Built by my friend . . .

Mrs Roly-Poly's fussing around out front. Grabbing baskets and drink and cloths and pushing Morris's wife ahead of her too. Making sure everyone gets a big serve of everything. No skinflinting when it comes to food. Eat as much as you can. Her reputation hanging on it. Do the Westalls know how to feed men or don't they? Tiger watching her. Keep the thing intact! Push out the fat pastries and the corned-beef and the loaves of bread and the fresh butter and the cucumbers and the tomatoes and lettuce and the scones and the cream and the whortleberry jam and the fruitcake!

Feast them!

And it's working. No one's saying a word. Everyone reaching for food and putting it away as fast as they can. Jaws doing all the work now. Cheeks bursting. Swallowing and chomping and gulping. All going at once. Eyes staring. Taking the edge off! The food disappearing faster than the stooks did.

And the Tiger squatting out in front of the whole show. His bum on the hub of a cart. And he's packing away a big share. Bullfrog! And he's still wearing his boss's jacket! A thick dark tweed with the temperature in the eighties. His notebook on his knee. He's starting to do a few sums. Adding and subtracting and dividing. Letting himself begin to *feel* the worth of it all. Giving his dreams some exercise. He doesn't want to sit in the shade. He wants to keep feeling the strength of the sun. He wants to see Solomon's carried and then it can rain. Too bad if it blasts acres of standing corn down the road. That's the way the market works. He licks his pencil and jabs another equation into his book. He's having fun. His mind far away. He looks up suddenly and catches me watching him.

Alsop comes round the corner of the rick and stops in his tracks. He's facing a solid wall of feeding labourers. Everyone looks at him. Saying nothing. Watching him to see what he'll do. The Tiger not seeing him yet. This hot cluster of sweating men jammed into the narrow lane of shade down the side of the rick not really interested in Alsop. But he's out there. Something different.

He doesn't see the Tiger.

Now he's lost confidence. On the point of turning away. Lacking the force to push in amongst us. Hesitating in the bright sun. Inexpert with his stick. Swaying and not actually going in any definite direction. His pale blue shirt and white trousers a weakness against the hard-worked field of shaved stubble and machinery. He could be swept aside by something. And it looks then as if he will collide with the tailgate of the waggon.

We stop chewing.

Waiting for the accident to happen as if nothing can prevent it. Feeling his pale forehead striking the metal. But Morris calls, 'Would you like a drink, Major?' And Alsop steadies himself, everyone chewing again, and he swerves in our direction. At the sound of Morris's call the Tiger looks round, intercepting Alsop. Taking over. And at once pushing food and drink at him and laughing.

Someone to crow to!

Swigging from his stone bottle of cold, bitter cider and thrusting it at the Australian. Aggressive. Powerful in sight of his men, his substance and all this energy directed towards his success. Stumped on the hub of the cart there in the sun. Sweating king bullfrog on his throne!

Wiping the neck with the palm of his hand. 'Here Major! Here! Drink!'

Alsop's overwhelmed. Pushed back. Can't resist him. He coughs and gulps and gets some of the vile stuff down. He'd sooner be drinking tea in the shade with someone reasonable. You can see that. But here he is instead and he can't escape. Drops splashing from the bottle onto his shirt. Someone laughs. No longer immaculate. The Tiger's excited, forgetting his manners and grabbing the bottle back. Taking a big drink. Who's Alsop anyway? And he's not talking, he's yelling. Bellowing. 'All set for the big stags then, Major?' And what's he saying? Alsop won't be hunting stags this autumn. Any fool can see that. Or ever again.

But it's just what he wants to talk about all the same. Tiger's hit the nail on the head. And Alsop dives on to the subject and snatches at it before giving himself time to think: 'Why don't you take Kabara along as your second horse to the Winsford meet next week?' he says.

Straight out like this it's too much for the Tiger. He's startled. As if he's been caught stealing something. And he slows right down at once. Comes to a dead stop. On guard. No longer the bullfrog, but wary now as a roused snake. He glances across at me. What's going on?

I don't want to know about it. I look away quickly and nudge Morris. 'We're getting there,' I say.

He stares out across Solomon's at the remaining stooks. 'We'll have her under the tin this evening,' he says, a little too serious. He doesn't look the best.

'You okay?' He doesn't answer me. Just smiles and gets on with his eating. Every now and then he stretches out his chin and drags in an extra-deep breath, then lets it out with a sigh. The stubble on his cheeks and the wrinkles under his eyes are lit up from underneath by the bright reflection of the day into our shade, and there is a dusting of tiny golden particles clinging like pollen to his eyelashes. 'You look tired.'

He turns to me: 'The boys are giving you a hard time on the elevator, eh?'

'I can handle them.' Morris laughs. We both know I can't handle them. We don't need to talk about it. I half listen to the Tiger and Alsop, fencing with each other now, circling around the business of Kabara. Both on to something very special. The Tiger holding a natural advantage and seeking to make the most of it. Probing around. Suggesting faults. Almost insulting the Australian. Rousing him . . .

The heat's coming out of my body and rising up in an envelope around me. A pie straight out of the oven! Spit would sizzle on me! But I can feel the strength flowing back with the food. Morris's wife comes over and pours us both some more tea. She kneels down, steadying herself with a hand on his knee. He watches her, and she looks at him when she's finished pouring. They don't say anything and Roly-Poly's calling out for something or other.

Alsop's voice is rising up, becoming more nasal as he gets excited. The Tiger's got him where he wants him. He's playing with him. Starting the squeeze. The Australian loud and foreign: 'Irish, Mr Westall! First-class Irish blood and not a fault in him!' It's true. Kabara's all that and more. Too good for the Tiger by a mile. No legitimate way a tenant farmer like Tiger can afford a piece of pure Irish bloodstock up to his weight; fifteen stone if he's an ounce!

'What are you saying, for Christ's sake?' Alsop affronted now. 'He was bred for one of your bloody dukes!' The Tiger making a laughable comparison with his own chestnut hunters.

'He's not an Exmoor hunter, Major,' Tiger says and whips out his watch, looking around, pretending to be getting fidgety for a start. But it's too early. The men are only now getting out their smokes. Tiger gets up and dusts himself off, he's going for the grease gun. 'You'll have a job selling him on the moor,' he says over his shoulder, moving off unexpectedly and leaving Alsop standing by the wheel. But Alsop's after him at once. Strident! Amazed! 'Who's talking about *selling* him?' The Tiger laughs and keeps going. Enjoying himself now. His instincts have got it right and he's opened the show on a hot note. He's got the man who wants to sell the horse chasing him!

'Take him to Winsford with you and give him a run. That's all I'm saying.' The crippled Australian lets the world know that he needs this sale badly. And if Tiger does take Kabara with him to Winsford next week, which is more than likely, because it doesn't look as though there'll be anything stopping him from going, it will look by then as if he's doing Alsop a favour. To some. There's a lot of screwing and grinding, undermining and probing, testing and poking into private situations, and there's a lot of shifting and shuffling around to be done before the Tiger parts with cash.

There he goes. Squirting grease again!

Alsop mopes along behind him, watching the stuff oozing out of the hot bearings and dropping in black sluggish blobs on to the stubble. He knows in his heart of hearts how badly the Tiger wants the horse and it's nearly killing him that he can't get any leverage on it. 'They don't look as though they really *need* greasing,' he says in the end.

The Tiger's hard at it, bum in the air and elbows going; 'They need it!' he growls, moving briskly to the next nipple and pumping.

So Alsop stands. Frustrated. Staring at the broad back of the Tiger ahead of him. No longer following.

He must feel me watching him because he looks across, directly at me. Shrugs and gives his head a shake, as much as to say, What can I do with a man like this?

I look away and drink some tea. It's a little late for him to be asking questions like that. I could have told him long ago. If he were smart he wouldn't be here. He'd be at home in Australia.

I'm enjoying watching the Tiger exulting. Digging himself confidently into this one! He should have got to know Kabara while he had the chance. But he let that slip and it's not going to be as easy now as he thinks. When it's too late it's going to hit him that he was right about one thing anyway; the horse may have the blood to give him superior speed and stamina, but it would take an extra-special horse-man to make an Exmoor deer-hunter out of Kabara.

It's a dream that's drawing him in now; seeing himself right up with the leaders, in at the death, going the distance in the winter with the hinds, when things get really tough, when only the fanatics, the silent obsessed hunters go out on the moor and pursue their crazy passions. Worse than gamblers! The old Tiger's been seduced by a dream: the greatest hunting farmer Exmoor's ever seen! And now here he is hooking himself firmly on getting a bargain out of Alsop's weakness. Sidetracked. Too smart for himself. He's going to have that stallion for a hunter! Well, let's see if he can coax Kabara across the bogs and channels of the Chains without coming to grief! Let him wade in! We'll see what happens. He's going to wish he'd forgotten all about Kabara and stuck to his chestnut nags.

But I shall say nothing. He is supposed to be the master of his situation.

A day off tomorrow. Everyone is going to the Winsford meet. So Morris and his wife are out there in the kitchen with the stove hot and a midweek bottle of stout between them. Something special. Nattering. The place is being torn apart by an Atlantic storm that came roaring in over Dunkery an hour ago and it's still pounding and ripping at this prefabricated junk heap. Blasting its way across the empty moor! My room's the place to be! Sitting on my bed with my legs drawn up and the eiderdown round my shoulders. Trying to read Ewart's *Elementary Botany*, and being distracted.

Boom! Crash! Smashing into the ridge! Inches away! It's a blitzkrieg! We're being pounded and deafened by the lightning explosions. Our ridge cops it. It's an attraction. A natural conductor. Bearing the full brunt of the ocean-bred storm. There's a piece of tin going smash, smash, smash on the roof but I can only just hear it for the wind.

But we haven't blown away yet!

And here comes the cold air. Whoosh! Like a big door opening and driving through the cracks and joints. There goes the last of the warm air!

The Tiger'll be over there all nicely tucked in with Roly-Poly, gloating on his good fortune. Every last scrap of his corn packed in under the tin. Safe and sweet. Acres of the stuff round here are being blasted into the mud tonight.

Well, too bad . . .

I keep looking at this same page without really taking it in: GYMNOSPERMS—*Pines, Firs, Larches, Yews, & Cycads. Synopsis of Description & Classification. The more important natural orders indigenous to Britain.* That's Ewart setting things up to be as exact as it is possible to be; scientific in other words. Leaving nothing to chance, hearsay or tradition. But checking it all out. Which is just what I want. I can do without guesses. Folklore, chit-chat, rumours, gossip. They've got all that stuff at their fingertips round here.

They know it, I don't.

It's imparted by word of mouth and sign language. You can never be quite sure what they mean. Nothing clear-cut and final about their answers. Everything's got to be spiced and packed and knotted up with ambiguities before they'll let you have it. And even then they grudge it. Ask them a straight question and they'll spit and cough and look over their shoulder, then say something you can't understand and move away. After he'd put the scythe into Solomon's the other day and we were all sitting under the hedge having a cup of tea, I asked Sam Jones how he'd cured the ringworm on the calves last year without ever coming near them. He breathed and wheezed and stared around, then mumbled, 'It's in the book,' before getting up and shifting himself.

Trade secrets I suppose.

I need opinion supported by evidence. Facts! And that's where my little stack of books comes in. They are a support to my thinking. And tonight I was going to read up on the larches. Find out something about those trees where the nott lives. But I'm not making much headway. And it's not only the storm that's preventing me.

The other big distraction is this: when I came into my room this evening, after our usual stewed steak and onions, potatoes, cauliflower and half a steamed pudding each, ready to set myself up for the night, I discovered that my resident rat had a companion. This gave me an unpleasant shock. It spoiled my mood. Botany for me is deciphering a code. I need all my wits for it if I'm not to miss the very point of significance that I'm searching for.

I had to kill the pair of them.

It's still preoccupying me.

A resident rat might sound ridiculous. Without explanation that's true of a lot of things.

When I first came here I couldn't work out for a while why Morris and his wife had put me in this room rather than in the room they use themselves. This bed that I'm sitting on is something special. It's not a bed you could go and buy in a shop. Someone has gone out of their way to build it. Not Morris. I've never asked him, but I feel sure Morris would not have constructed this bed. Her father maybe. As a dowry. Couldn't afford anything else so made something. A work of skill and love. No holds barred. Really go to town and make a bed like nobody's got. He would have had to bring the timber for it in here. There's no way you'd get this bed out of the room without ripping out a wall. Solid walnut. A local tree. There's walnut trees all over the place round here. Stolen, I imagine. No one's going to give that timber away. The square end-posts are nine inches through and nearly as tall as me! It's not a rich person's bed. It's a giant labourer's dream bed. Square, heavy and solidly made. Cut, sawed and morticed. Nothing turned, dovetailed or inlaid. No 'lines'. The headboard is one solid plank two inches thick and four feet deep. Finished with an adze. The whole thing rubbed with a hot mixture of boiled linseed oil and beeswax. As soon as I open the door in the evening, linseed. And no springs or wires. Cross joists and planks!

And her mother, I suppose, made the furnishings for it. The mattress is stuffed with half a ton of down. It's deep and warm and it smells of comfort. Then there's the bolster, the four pillows and this eiderdown. All huge and all filled with down.

My bed is a place of luxury.

There's nothing else like it in this house.

They have an ordinary double bed with a wire spring. Something for two bodies to lie on. Side by side. But not this one. This bed is my home roost. When my time's my own and I'm not out exploring the moor or checking on the nott, this is where I retreat. Everything on to the bed! Tip out my whole box of books. Spread my papers and rubbish around and wrap myself in the eiderdown. And if nothing out of the ordinary occurs I'm settled in for a good time.

Giggling and leaping around the other side of the wall used to go on nearly every night. Difficult to ignore. Lately it's more likely to be Morris coughing. Then murmuring to each other in the middle of the night and creaking and moving around. Restless. Morris not able to sleep. Then lighting up a smoke and coughing some more. Her telling him to get back into the bed. He's worked out, that's the trouble.

They're not having the fun they once had. Not as calm as he used to be. Irritable with the Tiger a couple of times this week. The truth is, he's not well.

One thing I've never heard them do in there, however, is kill a rat. They never get rats in their room. For myself I reached an accommodation with the rats the day I decided extermination was not the only way to deal with them. That arrangement has only just broken down tonight.

It's not just this bed that's all right with me. It's been the room too. I've always trusted what goes on in here. For example, I don't use the savings bank in the village shop. That way I also avoid having to put up with the tribal reactions to me of the rosy old fogies who inhabit the place. I keep my money in this chest of drawers here. Fifty-seven pounds so far. Pressed under my clean breeches.

It's a good feeling to have that hidden pile.

Another backstop.

Necessity. A pair of new boots once a year and a book every now and then, when I get to the market in Taunton with Tiger. That's all I spend money on. I don't take extended holidays, just the one-day kind. No one else round here takes extended holidays either. But I am expected to. 'So I suppose you'll be going off, then? For a week or so?' The Tiger starts enquiring hopefully as soon as Christmas gets close. Trying to coax me into it. And Morris and his wife, though they don't say anything, would be glad if I did. They don't like having me hanging around at Christmas time. It makes them uneasy. They think I haven't noticed, but the truth is they would like to get rid of me. Have a break from me for once. Forget I exist.

Once the general work comes to a stop things change for me. I don't fit and it's obvious. There's no covering it up by keeping busy. I'm a stranger in the middle of what's going on. An irritation. Irksome. Spoiling everybody's fun.

Morris may be from Wiltshire but he's still the son of Tiger's sister. He is related. And he married a local. All this doesn't make *him* a local, but it gets him a place in the goings-on. Intimacies and celebrations. Ritual!

And that's what I don't have and can't fake.

Christmas leaves me sticking up on my own in the middle of nowhere. They're surprised when they come across me. You can almost hear them saying it: 'What's *he* doing here?' People I've never seen before milling around in the kitchen wearing their Sunday best. Pushing. Yelling. Touching each other. Embracing and swaying, all talking at once. Keyed up and excited. Ready for something out of the ordinary. Snatching the first drink and downing it. In the mood for fun. They're not sure what they might get around to doing before it's over and this half scares them. Especially the men. The smoke and the beer and the noise!

A chance to go crazy.

I can't hide in here all the time. I have to eat and that's when I get stuck with them. I put up with it till one of them starts showing aggression: 'What's the matter with this one? Frightened his face'll crack if he smiles?' What can I say to that stuff? It embarrasses Morris. He's wishing I wasn't there. Hoping I'm not going to answer back and let one thing lead to another. Hoping things will go off well. No trouble. No hitches.

So I head off.

Out on to the moor. Down the combes and into the woods. Roaming or sitting still somewhere. In the frost with the naked trees against the moon. Smelling the cold clean earth. Giving my brain a chance to clear.

They feel better when they know I'm not here. Relieved. After all, who wants a stone-face sitting in the circle of good-timers? They want to zip along in their lingo without having me or the boss or anyone else checking on them. It's as simple as that. I hold them up. Keep the brakes on their excitement. They want to blast ahead and dribble and yell and do whatever comes into their heads. A waste of good beer otherwise!

Out in the wilderness with the Australians! That's where I am at Christmas time. Where Alsop and his missus are all the year round. Foreigners! The three of us! Except *he's* forever trying to find ways of winkling himself into the goings-on. She doesn't seem to care one way or the other.

We never see her. Or maybe she's more like me. But he'd love to be a part of it. Before the accident he'd stand around praising things when there was nothing to be said. Pretending to be impressed with everything he saw. Too loud. Being met with silence. But really just like me at party time. In the way!

And he still hasn't totally learned his lesson. I was watching him from the window here only this evening, before the storm broke. He came poking up along the road from Gaudon Manor. Lanky, alone as always, and bent by his pain. No hat. He stopped outside the gate here and stood jabbing the ground with his stick. Turning stones and whatever. The way he's seen Tiger do it. Except when the Tiger jabs this soil he's jabbing his own bones. Hardly knows he's doing it. Listening for the sounds of winter coming or something. You wouldn't know. Talking to his ancestors maybe. Nothing he'd admit to anyway.

It's no good Alsop trying stunts like that.

He's out there by the gate, hanging around for a minute or two, hoping Morris is going to see him and yell out a greeting. I could see he almost decided at one stage to come in and knock on the door. Hungry for a bit of company. But there's no place for him here. He heads off eventually, towards the pub at Handycross. Going that way. Probably nagged at home. Rather different from all the leaping and prancing he used to go on with. He's getting a lift to the meet with Morris in the morning. That should raise a few eyebrows among the locals. And might even cause some tension here too. Morris's wife's not going to feel like taking a back seat to the major. But he must reckon he's got to be there in person to see the Tiger in action on Kabara. Not ready to trust any second-hand accounts of the run. Wanting ammunition in favour of the horse so he can argue his case.

But he's lost that one already if he only knew it, and he might as well forget strategy. When the Tiger buys Kabara he'll do it on his own terms. If I were Alsop I'd be planning an orderly retreat from England, and thinking of getting back to my own country.

This is just the way it goes when I'm alone in here reading. I start following up on whatever's going on, if I'm not too tired, and I don't notice what's happening under my nose, right here in my room. Which is how I got taken totally off-guard by the rats the first time.

The book I was reading that evening was something special. It is lying here on the bed now in front of me. It is *The Master of Game* and was written by King Edward III's grandson in 1406. My copy was printed in 1909 and what's left of the cover is grey-green cloth with a gold medieval design. It is inscribed on the front endpaper: 'Peter Staines, on his twenty-first birthday, With best wishes from Sir Guy & Lady Fentner; June 1923.'

It smells wonderful!

Its author was the leader of England's vanguard at the Battle of Agincourt. He was killed there. Smashed aside by a great blow from an iron mace. So there he was, the leader in a fight that people have called England's greatest victory! And the same man sat down and wrote this book, which is gentle and well mannered, thoughtful and filled with elegant phrases and descriptions. He calls it 'My litel symple book.' He was too modest. It's not so simple, but is full of knowledge and feeling and understanding. He is writing about his passion, hunting. And he only writes what he knows, leaving conjecture to those who don't know. It is a book that I can open at any page and begin reading with pleasure. This is not hearsay; it's clear he has trodden through the high wet bracken on chill mornings and held in his hand the red earth where the fox has dug freshly. And his admiration for this animal, which others considered vermin, was keen. He says, 'The fox does not complain when men slay him, but defendeth himself with all his power while he is alive.' Some compliment from a warrior!

And there I was, right in there with the intimate thoughts of this Plantagenet, seeing him defending himself at his last battle without complaining of his wounds and without crying out, but doing his best and dying there. Settled deeply into my downy palace here, visions of Agincourt and the fox all mixed up and stewing around in my head, when I felt a slow, gentle pressure being exerted at the back of my shoulder, close up to my neck.

I looked at the door, moving only my eyes, thinking it just possible that my absorption in the book had been so great that I hadn't noticed someone come in and go round behind me. Some kind of local joke maybe? I was naïve enough then even to consider the possibility that I might be initiated into the ways of the locality. I was in a mood for odd things to happen to me anyway. After all, what was I to expect from these people? But in the stillness, during that couple of seconds, I heard Morris and his wife making their little noises behind the wall. There was no one with me.

And then the pressure eased, allowing me to hope that I might have imagined it, or maybe had one of those involuntary muscular contractions that feel just like a touch.

I was about to reach up and give my shoulder a rub when there it was again. Slow and easy but unmistakably something on the eiderdown. I leaped up and away from the bed, ready to keep going right through the door and all the way back to London. And a rat dropped off my shoulder and sat there, embedded in the warm folds of my eiderdown, from where it gazed at me.

I got such a fright that I panicked and grabbed one of my boots and pounded it where it crouched. It didn't try to get away and it didn't defend itself, but it seemed to resist the blows for ages. It took a long time to die. It hung on. Sight was in its gaze for so long that I almost despaired of killing it. I'd never killed anything before, not a decent-sized animal anyway, and hadn't realised quite how committed and violent it is necessary to be.

That was number one. There were plenty more to follow. And it wasn't long before I became a skilled and efficient rat killer.

Due to a continuous damp seepage there's a rotten area of skirting board and flooring in the corner under the chest of drawers. I've blocked it fifty times. But they keep at it. Nibbling and gnawing and scratching away all through the night, night after night until one of them gets through.

And it's just one. You'd think they'd come pouring in by the hundred. Rat waves squealing and shrieking after all that hard work. And I used to lie awake waiting for that grey avalanche. But it's just one. Quietly. Sits there on the floor in the open. No attempt at being sneaky about it. They are big, slow and easy to kill. Waiting for it almost. Making no attempt to dodge the blow. Not retreating back through the hole. Not a flicker of fight in them. Nothing of the Plantagenet or the fox about these things. Almost as if they had been sentenced. Listed for this hole. So I killed them for a while, but there was no sport in it. It was repetitive, predictable, unpleasant.

It was butchery.

And it soon began to depress me, but I kept doing it. It got harder and harder to deliver the death blow. I developed a muscular reluctance, a stiffness and uncertainty, which caused me to miss my aim altogether sometimes, or what was even worse, to botch the job and smash one of the doomed creatures across the back. I tried to stir them up, to put some fight into them, to give the dismal business an element of variety at least. But no matter what I did, jabbing and poking and yelling at them, they remained unmoved. Puddings. At most I could detect resentment, but never any actual resistance.

After a few months of this it got to the point where I'd come in and do various things around the room before killing the rat. 'I can see you,' I'd say, and then I'd get on with whatever it was I had in hand. Putting off the disgusting business. But sooner or later I'd have to make up my mind to do it. Go and get the stick and stand there looking at the one whose turn it was that night. It wasn't easy. In fact it gave me the creeps.

And it only got worse when I started discussing the business with them. Little black beady eyes looking up at me. Not so ugly really. Grey feet and that rodent tail. I've seen worse looking things. 'All right, you've got another fifteen seconds,' and I'd start counting slowly. Seeing the rat, intact, healthy, a reasonable rat life ahead probably, except for this situation. 'Okay, another half minute. But then I'll really have to do it.' Time running out. Then slam with the stick. One vicious smash on the head and they'd be dead, give a couple of kicks and I'd pick the limp carcass off the floor and carry it out by the tail. Chuck it on Morris's neatly maintained heap of pig shit up at the end of the garden. When Morris and I went past on the way to milking in the morning the bodies were always gone. Food for nocturnal owls and foxes . . . And if Morris and his wife were still up, sitting in the kitchen when I went past, dangling my dead rat, we'd nod an acknowledgement at it and say nothing. It put a blight on my evenings, however, wondering every night when the scratching and gnawing and squealing was going to result in a breach in my blockade. Coming in here after washing my feet, all set for an evening's reading, and finding this nasty job to be done.

I got sick of it. So one evening I pretended there wasn't a rat there, squatting silently under the chest of drawers, watching me. I got on the bed and started reading. 'The execution takes place at dawn,' I said, when it was time to snuff the candle out. And I lay down and had an undisturbed night. But of course when the morning came I was in my usual hurry. Woken by Morris's careful, knock, knock, knock on the wall. A cup of tea and a piece of bread and butter waiting for me. Just time to gulp it down while I laced my boots before we were off, out into the icy wind and the darkness, hurrying up the garden and across Old Ley to the farm.

I was well into the milking before I remembered the rat. But there was no chance to kill it when we got home for breakfast. It would have meant taking my boots off and disrupting the routine. By the time Morris and I get back for breakfast his wife has got control of the place. We're only in for a quarter hour; down our food and grab our lunch packs and we're out again.

So the rat was still in here when I got back that evening. *Still* in here, or in here again? I didn't know. It was more or less in the same position, keeping low and still, down there next to the hole. Looking sleepy, but watching.

I didn't say anything to it that night. I wasn't voicing any decisions, I mean, about what was going to happen. But I left it there. I did nothing and said nothing.

It would have been a week or so before I started coming up with things like, And what sort of a day have *you* had? when I got in at night.

My nights were peaceful. No gnawing and squealing going on behind the skirting board! No need to wonder if tonight was the night for rat killing! It was a relief. A new era. And I was beginning to feel grateful to the resident for sitting there quietly guarding that hole. I made one or two concessions. I called this one the Resident, and I gladly ceased to be the exterminating angel.

I believed in our unwritten agreement. He got the floor under the chest of drawers, I got my peace of mind. It was fair. And I like things to be fair. So I stopped worrying about the whole business.

Until tonight.

A situation foreseen by Morris.

Crouching in the straw, trying to keep our feet out of contact with the black ice on the frozen cobbles for a spell, down there in the disused threshing barn last winter, eating our lunch, I explained about the Resident. Morris listened till I'd finished. Nodding along with what I had to say. It was about week three of my new peace of mind and I was feeling very pleased with myself. Telling Morris was, in a way, a boast as much as anything. Like indicating that if he and his wife had been on to this, they wouldn't have had to move out, but could have gone on enjoying the luxury of their bridal bed. If that's what it is.

Morris didn't say anything. I suppose he'd noticed that I hadn't been carrying out any rats for a few weeks. And when I'd finished he lovingly sliced a segment from his portion of back fat, white, almost luminous stuff, turning it between his greasy thumb and forefinger, examining it with the eye of a specialist, before putting it in his mouth and chewing. His pocket knife poised over the remaining chunk.

When he'd swallowed the fat and washed it down with a mouthful of cold tea, Morris said, casual and interested, 'What will you do if the Resident gets a companion?'

It took a while. But there they were tonight. And squatting outside the limits of the chest of drawers! I was shocked. I felt betrayed.

'So this is the thanks I get is it?' Crazy! Fancy expecting gratitude from a rat! I'm out of practice and they dodged around. It was messy. But there was nothing else for it.

I couldn't have them setting up a new colony right here in my room!

Anyway, they're both out there on the dung-heap in the rain now.

Maybe Morris will help me to find a permanent solution. Then again, maybe there's really no such thing as a rat-proof house. Things aren't going to be the same in here . . . And there he goes now, laughing with her in there, then cough-cough-cough! The storm's letting up. Blowing itself out at last. It's late and my candle's burnt down almost to the tin, the flame wobbling madly, rearing up wide and yellow then almost snuffing itself, filling the air with the smell of candle grease and reminding me of the shelter and the air raids. All that old stuff coming up.

The hole's still there. I haven't tried to block it. It's silent too. I wonder what'll happen now? Just keep up the war I suppose. The rats won't stop. They're congenital colonists. That's biology.

I'd better get some sleep. I have to be up and out of here before Morris in the morning. I put a set of new shoes on Kabara and Finisher, the gelding, in preparation for today. The Tiger'll want them saddled and waiting by daylight at the latest. It's a long ride to Winsford from here.

The scent will be deadly after this storm!

Morris and his wife aren't awake when I slip the latch on the back door and step out into the darkness. The moon is still bright enough over the oaks in Will's wood to cast their shadows across the close-cropped turf of Old Ley. Everything's sodden from the storm and the air is cold and still.

I stand on the crest of the ridge and look down into the valley without a name that locals call the Black Valley, and I can see across a vast sweep of sleeping countryside all the way to the silvered waters of Bridgwater Bay and the outlet of the Doniford Stream. Everything is cool and clean! I can taste the air on my palate! There's the sound of water trickling out of a pipe under the hedge next to me. I have to go. As I turn I startle a blackbird from its roost and it flies out, flat and fast across the field.

From fifty yards away the farm could be abandoned. Dead. Deserted. A settlement left over from another era. The big dark shadows of the cattle shed, the barn, the stable and the house all joined together, their windows and doors facing inward to the yard. Blank walls to the world. Compact against storms and trouble, and against anything else that might come along. Expecting the worst. Their weathered grey featureless stone walls and their grey slate roofs not interested in anything outside. They don't want to know about it. Keep out! Silent in the autumn moonlight. Been standing there since who knows when? The odd bulge of the disused bread-oven poking out in to the road like the bum of a giant squatting in the end wall of the house.

I've got a good two hours of work to get through before daylight. Finisher and his mate Ashway hear me opening the road gate and they whinny softly. This is enough to start the cows moaning, even though they know it's too early for them yet. I light the kerosene lamp in the stable and close the door behind me. The soft light reveals the cobbled floor and the ashen stall-trees, their wood polished to a deep honey gloss by the rubbing of generations of hunters and plough horses. It's warm in here. The air rich with the acid smells of horse dander, piss, dung and meadow hay. Kabara is stationary in the shadows. Watching me. Making no welcome. The two geldings lean out and stretch for my hands, glad to see me. Ashway's not coming with us. I'll be riding Kabara, and Tiger will begin the day on Finisher. I get on with feeding them before I do anything else. Kabara and Finisher will need time to eat their fill.

Kabara's edgy. His breathing is noisy and shallow. It's the first time he's spent the night here and he knows there's something unusual being organised. He's not sure what's going to happen to him. But it's not only that. It's me too. I just hope he got some rest during the night. He's watchful. Staring at me and reacting to my every move. Maybe I should let the Tiger know that he has misjudged this stallion's temperament. Try and explain to him how it's come about that he's made this mistake. Do it in a way that doesn't make him feel that I'm questioning his judgement. Maybe this great horse could come to some harm? I know Kabara's capable of deciding that no one's going to get near him. He's capable of extreme behaviour, of forgetting all his schooling and deciding things for himself. In other words, of being so strong about his life that he becomes a rogue stallion. A danger. And you may as well call that the end of him. But how would I approach the Tiger?

I clean out Finisher's stall first. Then I go over with my dung-fork and unlatch Kabara's door. He's shown no interest in his feed. He is totally alert and on his guard. I hesitate to go in there with him. For almost two months I've taken his trust for granted. Now he's withdrawn it. For the moment anyway, and I'm afraid of him. He keeps moving around, shifting his weight from side to side and from his front legs to his hind legs with a stiff series of short movements. Continuously positioning and repositioning himself, in any split second ready to strike.

I don't want to die yet but I've got to get in there and clean out his stall. 'Everything's just normal,' I say, 'so there's nothing to worry about,' and I edge in through the half-door. My voice sounds watery. I latch the door behind me and we look at each other . . . 'I haven't been completely honest with you have I?'—this is not an easy conversation to get started. I feel guilty for some reason. As if these difficulties are my doing—'There's nothing I can do about the Tiger,' I say, starting to fork out the soiled straw bedding closest to the door, picking the clean stuff out and tossing it to one side, his eye following every movement. 'He's like you. He can't be told. He's got to make up his own mind. And anyway something had to happen didn't it? I mean Alsop's no good to you any more, is he? You've got to be sold and bought and moved around and all that stuff. Haven't you? You can't just sit over there at that place for the rest of your life.' Talking is making me feel better. I'm not so scared. And Kabara's tossing his head and snorting at the sound of my voice, instead of jerking around with that menacing insect intensity. It's an improvement. But I know the truth is really that his history's not working out well for him. He shouldn't be skulking around down here between these old farm walls. There's not enough room, here in this situation, for him to recover from the sort of mistakes he might get forced into. There's nothing grand to meet him on his own ground. He should be standing at a great stable where he'd get his chance to be compared with the best.

But the Tiger's seen *his* chance.

By the time I've cleaned his stall and chucked in a heap of fresh oaten straw Kabara's settled down enough to let me start grooming him. I get going on him with the rice-root brush. I have to leave him standing free. I have a feeling he wouldn't put up with cross-ties anyway. I've never tried tying him down or restricting him in any way. I'm no horse-master and couldn't get him to do something he didn't want to do. It's always his decision that settles things one way or the other.

When I've been over every inch of him with the soft brush I get started on the part he enjoys the most. I rub him vigorously with the palm of my hand, generating heat and bringing his body oils to the surface so that his fine raven coat will glow with all the midnight colours, blue and green and purple in the sunlight! He half closes his eyes and begins letting out the odd moan of sheer pleasure. And I'm grunting and sweating with the effort. Pushing my palm deep into his splendid muscle, holding myself against him with my other arm in order to keep my balance, and begin-ning to wonder what our disagreement was all about a minute ago. I tell him how beautiful he is. How everyone will stare at him and admire him and fear him. And when I'm doing his shoulder he reaches round and starts grooming me too. I get to work on his full mane then. Hand-picking every hair of it. Strand by strand. Damp-ening it with water where it needs it so that it will all fall on the near side. And finally back to his coat again. A last polish with a lightly oiled rag, smoothing it with the sweep and direction of the hide and bringing out the highlights under the yellow flame of the lamp. Reaching under his tail and down between his thighs, wiping the tense and bulging globes of his testicles, him grunting and tucking his belly—each ball the size of my clenched fist!—and on down his thighs, in behind the powerful muscles of the stifle and the gaskin, his legs planted firmly. Like polishing living gateposts! Back up over his croup and under the tail, and he's tucking and wincing again. All that power there for breeding! How much is the Tiger going to insure these ballocks for? If he actually gets to own them?

I get down and start crawling around under his belly. A minute and thorough check of his legs. Looking for anything I might have missed while grooming him, any small sign of a hurt or something that could be a problem starting to show up. But he's clean. He's begun feeding, lipping the sweet milled oats and the delicious flakes of linseed cake.

We're friends again.

I stand and watch him for a moment, relaxed, within striking range of his deadly hooves. And I try to imagine myself telling the Tiger when he comes out all geared up and ready to go hunting this morning: 'Listen, Boss! This horse is too good for you. You're not up to him! He'll get you into trouble!' I can see him standing there calmly listening to all that coming from me! Advice on horse business to the Master! *Me* telling the Tiger how to lead his life!

I leave the black horse to it, give him a chance to get a decent feed into himself, and I go in and give Finisher the treatment. What a contrast! I head for the cottage then, for a quick breakfast and change. Morris is having a lie-in. She's given him his breakfast in bed and I can smell the smoke from his cigarette coming down the passage. He's making the most of it. Sitting up in bed enjoying himself before he has to get over there and get on with the milking. He won't mind doing it on his own this morning. He'll take his time. It's still early now, but he's behaving as if it's late. Letting himself feel the holiday.

I'm starving and the bowl of thick porridge is good. I scoop on heaps of cream and sugar! I'd rather have more porridge, but as soon as I've finished she puts down a plate of fried bread and home-cured bacon in front of me. It's vaguely warm. Been dished up for half-an-hour and sitting on the side of the stove. It's something of a drawback, this stuff. That pig again! I wait till she's not looking and then I cut out the areas of blue. I don't know what causes this deep-blue spotting close to the rind; something to do with the action of the brine, or the copper rivets in the barrel, I daresay. It looks like the bluestone, sulphate of copper, that we put on the sheep to cure foot-rot, and it tastes so bad that it lingers on my tongue for hours. I have to face up to it every morning. She doesn't like to see any part of that pig being wasted. It irks her. Goes right against her grain. It's something she can't relax about. They put a lot of care and hard work into fattening that thing up each year, and the way it all turns out after it's been cut up and put into the barrel is a point of pride with her. She can't help feeling criticised by the way I treat it. She's never said anything, she stops short of nagging me, but she hates to see me picking and poking around with it instead of just gulping it down the way Morris does. I'm not expected to go into ecstasies over it, she's not an idiot, but I am supposed to enjoy getting bacon with bits of poisonous blue stuff in it.

I hate to offend her.

And this time she catches me trying to slip some of it into my pocket. Well that's too bad. She pretends she hasn't noticed and asks me if I want another cup of tea.

But I've had enough.

I dive into my room and put on my clean pair of breeches. I'm not finished over there yet and time's getting on. As I head back across the field the sky is a streaky grey over the Quantock Hills and the light is on in the farm-house. Going into the yard I can hear the Tiger down towards the orchard feeding his sows, squealing and screaming and yelling going on. And the Diplomat's woken up too, the slow smash of his horns on the tin going for another day.

It's time for me to saddle up.

The Tiger gets extra-finicky on hunting days. And today more than ever, with his first ride on the noble stallion in the offing.

Ashway watches us while I put the gear on the other two. He knows all about it and wishes he was coming with us. There's everything you can think of to go on Kabara, and it's not a straightforward business to get it adjusted correctly. The long-shanked pelham bit with a curb mouthpiece belongs to Alsop. It's a severe piece of equipment if you want it to be, and in the excitement of hard riding it's easy to hurt the horse with it. For maximum comfort it's got to sit just nicely behind his incisors, but low enough so that his lips aren't drawn back by it. I take plenty of time to set it just right, making sure the feeling of it in his mouth doesn't make him want to chew and tongue it in order to try to get it into a more comfortable spot. I like to see his head still, his gaze relaxed, and no distractions. The Tiger has made up his mind that he wants a standing martingale rigged on him too. But this is not necessary either to improve his bearing or to control him. Kabara's stance is without fault, he flexes at the poll naturally and from pride, giving the appearance of alertness and intelligence; a naturally aristocratic bearing. The martingale will irritate him and complicate matters if anything does happen to go wrong. Getting into difficulties on a horse that's got straps and buckles and extra bits and pieces of harness hanging all over it is more dangerous than if he's only wearing a saddle and bridle.

But it's the Tiger's way to tie things down.

I leave the martingale as loose as I dare. Even then it's a distraction for the big horse. Whichever way I look at it, the Tiger's going to tell me to tighten it a notch or two, so the looser the better to begin with. Finisher's harness falls into place of its own accord. Always adjusted to the same holes, the dark wear-bars across the leather tell me exactly what to do. But with Kabara it's still a matter of style and opinion at this stage. Like his ownership, unsettled. No routine to call on. Anybody's guess you might say, and one idea pretty much as good as another.

We're ready at last.

I lead them both out into the yard by the bridles. And we wait. The three of us. Facing the closed kitchen door. Me in the middle. On parade! I'm wearing my cap, my Harris tweed jacket and my clean corduroy breeches. I've given my leggings and boots a rub with hoof oil. Not too bad!

There should be someone to take our picture!

It's a masquerade for me.

And here he comes! Right on cue! Flinging the kitchen door open and striding towards us. Backed up by Roly-Poly standing in the doorway and with her arms folded. Expecting the worst. Hoping for it! And he's not carrying his stick. It's his riding-crop this time.

'Good morning, Boss.'

Wearing his pale, fine-twill tailored breeches with the expensive buckskin strapping. Black bowler, brown boots and leggings and a coat and tie. His coat done up by the top button, showing most of his waistcoat underneath, tight over his gut. It's the tailored breeches that are a sign to those who know! Too smart for a tenant farmer. A giveaway to his secret dreams! That other person; hunting squire Westall!

He's gone round behind us without a word. But I know exactly where he is because Roly-Poly's following him every step of the way with her toad-wife gaze. She's all set to start tut-tutting and ooh-aahing and nodding her squat head the minute he finds something wrong with the way I've done things.

Not a word out of him yet!

I'd like her to be disappointed.

We have never spoken to each other. I tried a 'good morning' on her once, but she looked away, letting me know she hadn't heard. And the time Morris and I shifted her hen houses for her she supervised the manoeuvre, which took us all morning. But she didn't speak to me once. Everything went through Morris. She even asked *him* if *I* wanted sugar in my tea! She's an extremist. A fanatic about what she holds to. And I'm a headache for her. A long-term illness. A nagging irritation. Something not right about the place. She feels in her bones that people like me and Alsop shouldn't be allowed. We ought to be banned if governments did their job properly.

And the truth is, I'm no use to her. She sees through me. Through the masquerade. I've got no right to love this country! It's hers! And if I weren't such a glutton for hard work she'd soon convince the Tiger to blast me off the premises. She's hoping for a big mistake from me. That's why she's watching the Tiger so closely now, working his way round these horses, inspecting! But not a word! He's tugging at this and poking and picking and pulling at stuff, lifting the saddle flaps, checking the billets, the girths, the stirrups, and who knows what else? He's leaving nothing to chance but he's still not finding anything to scream about. And here he is, by my elbow, at the throat-latch at last, jiggling the martingale under Kabara's neck, the horse eyeing him, tense, ready to react.

'Tighten it!'

I do as I'm told and he hands me his rolled riding mac to tie on behind Finisher's saddle. Then he bids me 'good morning'.

It's time to mount up.

Morris must have come in without me noticing him. He's left the road gate open and I see him now going across the yard with a barrow load of chopped mangolds for the cows. He looks across at us, pausing to watch the Tiger, who is dancing around with one foot in the stirrup, the other hopping, striving to swing his bulk into position. Not a lot of bounce in him. He'd take a chop at me with his riding-crop if I dared offer my assistance. And it's not much good me mounting up till he's firmly in the saddle. So I watch him, like Roly-Poly and Morris, and Kabara too. We all watch him grunting and striving and hopping around, dragging at Finisher so that the horse is forced to shift his stance in order to keep his balance, and it's this shifting and shuffling that's frustrating the Tiger.

'Stand! Damn you! Stand!'

Finisher tossing his head and snorting, feeling his oats and half enjoying the struggle. Then with a mighty heave the Tiger's swinging through the air, his right leg flying out into space and carrying him past the point of no return, Finisher skittering aside and ducking away! We're holding our breath! All I can see is the Tiger's enormous bum with the fine twill stretched bone-tight across it. He seems to be floating through the air, going the wrong way. Then Finisher coils back under him.

And the Tiger's up!

A hand to his bowler, a haul on the reins, a couple of kicks and he's a young man again! Up there! In command! A solid horseman growing out of the powerful horse's back! He won't come off unless Finisher falls. The Tiger is a fearless rider once he's up. He is never reckless, just unafraid, and he will use Finisher to the utmost of the horse's strength. He is a commander now! A director! And that's that! Free and big and strong and not old any more once he's up there, and he will put up with no resistance to his commands nor to any mistakes in carrying them out, and he will resort to his spurs and to his whip without hesitation. And there he is now, sorting out Finisher's ideas about pig-rooting, holding the gelding's head up and keeping him high on the toes so that he can't set his weight squarely on to his hind legs. And the Tiger's smiling with delight! Exercising his technique! He's not a tenant farmer any more. Now he is *a horseman*! There is his own judgement in these matters, and there is the great strength and fitness of the animal under him. He is sure of both. And all this has suddenly engrossed him with his own will and happiness. His eyes are brighter. The blood is freshening his complexion. His heart is beating faster and he loves it all so well that he looks down at me from the height of his wonderful prancing perch, and he laughs. He can't help it. The laugh escapes from him. 'Get up, boy! Get up!' he calls to me with great enthusiasm. And he snaps his reins and he wheels his mount and he trots briskly across the yard and out of the gate.

Roly-Poly turns and goes into her kitchen, closing the door. And Morris bends to grasp the handles of the wheelbarrow. He lifts it, and looking at me, he smiles: 'See you at Winsford.' And away he goes, ducking his head and disappearing into the dim interior of the cowshed. I lead Kabara out on to the road, closing the gate before mounting. My heart, too, begins to beat faster as I turn him right-handed along the high-banked viewless road that twists and turns and meanders about, heading through the rich red farmland towards Wiveliscombe and the moor beyond. The Tiger's already out of sight and so I lift Kabara into a trot. We have twenty-five miles to ride to the meet.

It's now that I can't help feeling anxious. Riding second horse is not the easiest thing in the world. Even for the local, with a life's knowledge of the moor and the habits of the wild red deer, it is a tricky business. And there is always the element of luck. Will things go my way today or not? Predicting the movements of the hunted deer and being in the right place when the fresh horse is needed, that's what it's all about. And most second-horsemen lead the second horse and ride a mount of their own. But Tiger can't afford that luxury. In fact this whole business is really beyond his means. It's stretching things. Keeping a pair of hunters, and taking me off the real work of the farm, is pushing his economy to the limit in anything but a year like this one has been for him. Now he's a gambler. He's won a big pot and he's feeling confident. But it's that silent look that Roly-Poly sent after him just now before she closed her door that tells the long-term story, the real story, you might say. It scares her to think he might buy Kabara with the surplus cash. She doesn't want this expensive black aristocrat lodged in her stables, any more than she wants me round the place. It all adds up to risks she can do without. She has in her mind the run of bad years that will come, sooner or later. In their cycle. And she wants everything to be in order to meet that day. Tight. No loopholes where fate, or something worse, might sneak through and turn a couple of bad harvests into a full-scale disaster.

But Tiger's the master.

And when it comes to hunting the deer he listens only to his heart. In hunting he seeks for perfection in himself.

There is no logic to it really. If you look at it calmly it makes no sense. And it affects me in its own way too. Hunting is not something that I would care to fail at. There are some things I don't mind making a mess of. But not this business. I see eye to eye with the Tiger on this one. Though I don't really know why I should.

I trot on after him. It is a fine clear day with only a light northerly breeze just starting to pick up now. There shouldn't be any rain unless the weather swings round to the west later in the afternoon, something it can almost be relied on to do around Dunkery and the Chains—I'll get gradually damp right down to my underpants through the day however, rain or not, for the bracken and ground-cover is at its height just now, and stays wet all day. Not to mention the foliage we'll be plunging through.

I give Kabara his head and we descend the hill, following the Tiger. And here the narrow road runs through Norton's Coppice. A deteriorated island of woodland this, its twisted undernourished limbs of thorn and oak too close together in places even for a horse to pass between them. An unvisited little wilderness on its own, probably generations since it was cropped for poles. The Tiger says, without explanation, that it's not fit ground.

I catch up with him where the road passes through this gloomy spot, and a yellow, long-legged vixen crosses just in front of Finisher, going home, pausing for a second or two to examine us before tucking her tail and bounding lightly into the wet underbrush. Her gaze in that instant revealing the mask of a harried and hungry animal, weary with age, her hunting unsuccessful.

Hearing me pounding up close behind him, the Tiger calls, '*Her* last winter coming up!' while keeping the Finisher going at a good fast trot through the puddles, muddying the hooves I've just oiled. We draw quickly up the hill together and out of the shadows of the coppice, passing Gaudon Manor on our left—the big house still showing no light—and then a quick left-hand turn off the cambered road and we're swallowed again, into the steep narrow tunnel of Will's Lane. Keeping to our pace and startling the birds with our sudden entrance, slipping and splashing on the exposed rocks where water is cascading from the field drains in solid streams, gathering at the bottom of the lane and flooding the grass, before flowing slowly away through Handon's cornfield—almost a lake. Here the storm has really done some damage. Nine acres of barley flattened into the earth. I'm almost going to yell out something but the Tiger bores ahead without a pause, square on his horse, looking neither left nor right, gaze scanning the ground ahead, sharp, saving his mount where he can and making the best time. Concentrated. Riding. No slowing down to look at lost corn. His mind on hunting now, not the miserable luck some farmers might have; neighbours or not. And we're past it.

Going on, we pass meadow after meadow all threaded with silver streams, down deep lanes, muddy and waterlogged, rutted, twisting, full of corners in endless meanderings— we cross the early-morning countryside. The Tiger attacks each bend and turn with confidence, taking a fork and wheeling at each junction—the entrances to some lanes are almost closed over with rank autumn growth; he rides without hesitation. As if it is all written in his brain; his ancestors treading and treading these tracks for a thousand years before him. We can never see more than a few yards ahead of us, except when we pass a gate or a break in the bank, and then the sweep of countryside is revealed for an instant. But there is no open road anywhere. No direct route going into the distance. The roads are forever coiling back on themselves. Aimless. Confusing and frustrating to any stranger trying to get from one place to another, but familiar to the inhabitants.

I follow the Tiger through this intimate labyrinth of his, not speaking, threading our way, the regular creak of our saddles and the splash of our horses' hooves accompanying us. I hold the big stallion a few paces behind Finisher, just out of range of the mud and water that he's throwing up, and we trot on, holding forward into the strengthening day, until the sun lights the golden beeches suddenly where they meet over our heads.

Time stands still after a while, and the regular rise and fall of Tiger's broad back and the bobbing black bowler ahead of me are hypnotic. It is the rhythm of the slap and splash of the hooves too. It could go on forever.

I don't know what I have been thinking about. In another world. Forgetting Winsford and the hunting ahead of us today, forgetting to be anxious about the way things will go. Daydreaming. For how long? Carried along securely by Kabara, his stride not faltering once. That's why I'm not a real horseman, letting my thoughts drift off like this, so that when the Tiger suddenly slows to a walk I almost come off as Kabara wheels to avoid Finisher's rump. I recover my seat, relieved the Tiger hasn't looked round. We have begun to climb. We have arrived at the edge of the valley—the boundary of the Tiger's labyrinth. We are at the foot of Ridge Hill.

Rising in front of us are the eastern ramparts of the moor.

Sensing hunting country under him Finisher snorts and shakes his head, stretching at the bit, keen to get on, and Tiger cautions him. Kabara has tightened up a little—taken himself in a notch or two. He doesn't snort or prance or attempt to increase his pace against the walk that Tiger is holding us to. But I feel a difference in him. Like the day I took him down the steep combe into the larchwoods, to the soiling pit of the Tivington nott, there's a balance in him now, an alertness, a readiness for action that is so well tuned that I am reminded again of how far I am outclassed by him.

As we ascend the long hill slowly (skirting the town of Wiveliscombe) and the rich red farmland drops away behind us, the weave of its ways laid out in a pattern below us, the breeze cools and shifts towards the west. We're coming into a wild uplifted landscape. It's not clover and turnips and wheat up here. We're finished with all that, farmers and crops. Up here it's great brakes of bracken, six foot high, dense, wet, concealing holes and old rubbish, abandoned junk and wire and God-knows-what else; deer even! Gorse almost as bad, and dominating everything the thick tussocky moor grass, criss-crossed with hidden channels and ancient peat diggings. We can't help becoming quieter, taking it more carefully, looking around, more intent now, more concentrated on this business that we're here for. Up there ahead of us there are vast tracts of heather and bog that have never been broken by a plough. Untouched! The way God left it, from here to the uninhabited Atlantic coast. We're entering the last ancient homeland of the wild red deer of England.

Coming over the crest at last we see a stony road stretching ahead of us, a wide-looping silvery-grey scratch diving and curving through the empty landscape, tussocks of flying bent as far as the eye can see, in flower, laying a purple mist over it all. We keep going, straight on, not pausing to look back over our shoulders at the view of the valley we've just left. Intent now on penetrating this place. There's no one about. It's quiet, empty, still. We'd better watch out. If we come to grief in this country we've got no one to look to but ourselves. It's true! We're intruders, outsiders, the Tiger as well as me, looming up suddenly over the crest from down below. And the inhabitants have seen us. They're on the defensive. They're wary. They know we're up to no good. So they're keeping out of sight. This stillness is not natural. They're holding their breath and hoping we'll just pass through. Hoping we'll keep going and let them get on with whatever it was they were getting on with before we appeared on the horizon; they know what to expect from men on horses.

We follow this unfenced road for over an hour, keeping our mounts at a good fast walk, and seeing nothing but the silent purple moorland all around us. There's a high, thin cloud forming as the sun climbs, and the steady north-westerly has a damp chill in it; ideal for hunting after last night's rain. Breaking the silence, Tiger says, 'It'll stay fine then.' Talking to himself. Not addressing me really, so I don't answer, just accidentally letting his private conversation with himself pop out. And that's about it for conversation all round, on this ride, until we begin to come down off the moorland and descend towards the steep wooded hill behind Winsford; at which point he says, 'Well, what's John Grabbe got for us today?' And leads me down, still at a walk, through the pinewoods and out into a field with four red cows in it. They watch us while we negotiate the gate, maybe hoping we'll forget to close it. And maybe nothing. Across this field and out a final gate, the hooves of our horses clatter on to the tarmac.

Around the bend to our right, coming down from their kennels at Exford, and filling the narrow road from bank to bank, is the pack of tall, solemn, heavy hounds. The red-coated huntsman is leading them towards us. As we come out the gate on to the road suddenly in front of them, every eye focuses on us; the unsmiling huntsman's too. Startled by this unexpected sight, Kabara backs off and lets out a tight, high-pitched sound, something of fear and aggression in it. And there *is* something frightening in the way they are coming towards us, tightly packed, mouths lolling, staring at us. I get the feeling they would hunt us. We wait for them to go by, giving them precedence, their due I suppose, and the huntsman nods, exchanging an off-hand and ungenial greeting with Tiger, preoccupied and talking to his hounds all the while, doing his job. It's only fear of him that's keeping them in check. He'd hang any one of them that got out of line, he'd do it now, this minute, without any discussion or second chances. He'd string it up by the neck in the hedge here, and they know it. But they're bred against control, they're bred to hunt to the limit, and that's what they'll all die doing. And they'll hunt anything he lets them hunt. In a pack or alone. They don't care. And *without* his permission if they can manage it. There's not much they're afraid of, these big lead hounds coming up now, in the front, each one capable of pulling down a full-grown stag— but they're afraid of *him.* They've known him from the day they were born and they know he has power over their lives; whether they live or whether they die, whether they hunt or whether they just long to, whether they eat or whether they starve, whether they breed or, in the end, whether they hang; it's up to him. Without him they're nothing.

I watch him talking to them all the time, speaking a private language that only he and they really understand. He doesn't greet me as he goes by in the lead, and I say nothing, just watch him. His hunting cap's jammed home tight on his small round skull and his big dog-ears are sticking out conspicuously, each side of his close-shaven head. His eyes are deep-set and almost completely hidden by the low peak of his hard cap, but you can tell by the resolute set of his lips that there's not a lot of humour in their expression; knowing, and keeping it to himself, that's what he's on about. And it's true, he's the only one, really, who can ever fully appreciate the performance these dogs put up, who can ever really know what it's all about. No one else knows them well enough. No one else is so far into it as he. So he's isolated by it, a knowing, superior solitude, alone with his hounds and his private understanding. They all look to him, the hunters, but it cuts him off from them, even from his employer, the master, and from the few really passionate devotees of this business. No matter how carried away *they* get, how deep into it they go, how great the risks they take, with their money or their necks, for them hunting's still *something else*. He and his dogs are in it together for life. There's nothing else for them, only this. It's not a game. It's life and death. And he, as well as his hounds, very likely despise everything else, except perhaps the high priest of it all, John Grabbe the harbourer. At any rate, Kabara and I are just obstacles in the road at this moment, something in the way to be got round; second-horsemen in the wrong place at the wrong time are one of the regular frustrations of his day!

I watch him going by, riding his scruffy-looking mare, Kit, his red coat faded, threadbare at the collar, and weathered to a smooth pale gloss by hard usage.

A grim little man.

Not daring to get ahead of him, it's not till he's gone past that the hounds come surging round us; on foot I wouldn't last a minute down there. Pressed to the side of the road, Kabara is unsteady for a moment, scrabbling for a secure footing and getting his offside feet onto the rise of the bank. I can feel his panic at being boxed in, and his anger too, mounting in a wave inside him as these heavy senior dog-hounds come up close on him, pushing and snarling and snapping and whining and sniffing and licking around his dancing legs. They are the mature survivors, these, of maybe four or five or even six seasons; many of them, by the law of averages, are facing their last season now. At their peak, each one is hardened to suffering, experienced in strategy, and bold and strong enough to stay with any deer to the bitter end. There has to be courage in this, but it goes deeper than courage; in this pack these hounds are the nobility. And Kabara hunches up as they touch him, sensing the menace in them, tightening the girth, his flanks quivering, I can feel him getting ready to strike, tuning his stance for it.

What a way to start the day!

I can sense the Tiger and the others off to my right, their attention directed at me and what I'm up to, but I haven't got time to check them out or pretend to be in control. I'm about to get tossed into that moving tonnage of hungry dog muscle! Bait! Kabara's forgotten I'm up here. He's on the point of snapping into a few high leaps and pirouettes! There's just a chance I could make it if I lunged off his back and dived into the centre of the hedge. And I'm measuring and considering this move when the huntsman's voice drifts back to his hounds and they back away, taking the pressure off, growling and complaining and reluctantly disengaging themselves from this interesting situation, reminded, at last, of their real business. They are followed by a rush of the rest of the pack; the eager younger dogs, the new entry, the less bold, the ones who still hope to become leaders and those who never will; and, skulking among this motley, those miserable survivors who once led and have since been deposed. Kabara steps out into the middle of this lot and rips out a piercing challenge, the stallion's whistling scream, sending these tail-enders scrambling for their lives.

'You'll watch where you're putting his feet, boy!' The Tiger, sharp, annoyed, coming up on me, accompanied by

Mathew Tolland the whipper-in, who's grinning. And they go past me, Tolland's voice coming back; 'Isn't that the Australian's black horse?' I don't catch the Tiger's response. It wouldn't be much. He won't be drawn on the subject of Kabara till he owns him. I have to laugh, though, at him thinking it was my mishandling of Kabara that nearly got us into trouble then, rather than the fact that I wasn't handling the stallion at all, that Kabara was making his own decisions and had forgotten I was on board. I keep to the middle of the road, talking to him, reassuring him, and myself. And the two second-horsemen come up on us and ride past, giving me a nod and looking at Kabara with interest. They're each leading an unsaddled horse, one for Jack Perry, the huntsman, and the other for Tolland. I fall in a few yards behind them.

Ten minutes later we ride into the village of Winsford. The stallion and I bringing up the rear of this little caval-cade. There won't be many here today who will have ridden as far as we have. Once over the bridge we follow the main road. It's a long, thin village, jammed tight up its narrow valley, overlooked by the steep, thickly wooded slopes of the moor, the River Exe down one side of the main street and houses down the other. It's only just after ten o'clock but already there's quite a crowd; cars parked each side of the road, and riders and people on foot wandering around in the middle. The locals out in force. A few tourists, labourers, housewives, kids and, of course, those who've come here specially for the hunting season. Not real hunters though, most of them, just people out for some fun; satis-fied if they happen to see a deer in the distance at some stage of the game; whether the one being hunted or not. And they're all milling around on the road together, getting in the way of single-minded Mr Perry and his hounds.

He'll be glad when the winter comes and hind hunting gets going. Then the only ones who come out in the bitter weather to bother him mean to ride with him to the death. I look out for Morris but I can't see him anywhere. The horse and I are jammed up close behind Tiger and the hunt staff as they pilot the hounds through; Perry's still out front on his own, keeping the leaders in a tight formation, making sure they are not distracted and that their minds stay focused on the serious business ahead of them. Tiger and Tolland yell out impatiently, 'Hounds, please!'

We're getting down towards the pub when, pulled up on the river side of the road, and a little apart from everyone else, or *given* a wider berth out of respect, there's the master's old black motor car, nose towards a fir tree, a small party of foot and horsepeople gathered around the open front door. Strapped securely on the back of the car is the massive wooden box for the stag's carcass. Perry and Tolland, the Tiger and the rest of them salute her as we go by, doffing their hats. I can't actually see her, she's obscured by the people around her. But I've seen her before. She'll be sitting on the front seat with a little table set out for her bits and pieces—a thermos of tea, binoculars, and one thing and another. Who knows what else? Her special things for the day. She'll be holding court. She is very old. And, according to Tiger and Morris and anyone else I've ever heard speak about her, she nurtures religiously the old ways of hunting. Do they mean the ways, I wonder, that are spoken of in *The*

Master of Game? Ways as old as that? Or older? I don't know. She's small and shrunken, always in need of being helped by someone else, and, no matter what the weather, is always dressed to the neck in dark green tweeds. She has been the master of these staghounds since long before anyone here can remember. She has outlived her own generation. One opinion is that when she dies true deer-hunting on the moor will die with her.

And there she is now! Being got out of the car and onto her feet to salute her hounds and her huntsman. She stands for a moment, unaided, alone, her right hand raised not much above the level of her shoulder. A stationary little figure, almost a head shorter than those who are standing around her, and while she looks towards Jack Perry and the hounds, it is at *her* that they are all looking. She is isolated for a moment with all these people looking at her, before her companions help her back into the car.

There must be some here today who wonder what to make of it all.

The three riders in her party mount up and head over towards us. One of them is Mrs Grant. I've seen her around often, a regular. And everyone knows the other two as well. The man about thirty or so on the blood bay stallion is Lord Harbringdon, and the big man on the huge grey gelding is Harry Cheyne, the chairman of the Hunt Damages Committee and a friend of the Tiger. Fanatics, anyway, the three of them. Cheyne urges his horse forward, bumping Mrs Grant's mount as he pushes through, but not apologising or even noticing, cutting straight across to us, clearing a swathe through the crowd in the road as if there is no one there—

too bad if someone gets trodden on—and calling out to the Tiger while he's still more than twenty yards off; 'A fair morning, Bill!' People can't help staring at him as he goes by, especially people on foot. He's something to see. Obviously a man of great physical strength and, even from a distance, there is a sense about him of impatience that is only just under control, as if he might go crazy if you made a real point of getting in his way. He surges forward and takes up his place smack in front of me, and right next to the Tiger, who offers him a du Maurier from his tin, and responds with: 'It's starting to look promising, Harry.'

They are happy to be with each other, these two, and for the Tiger this is his most cherished friendship. A lot of people, besides the Tiger, admire Harry Cheyne, and there are quite a few who can't stand him, but for the Tiger there's something more complicated than admiration in it . . . I see Harbringdon and Mrs Grant still picking their way across, taking it easy, in no big hurry, exchanging a greeting here and there as they go by, acknowledging the social nature of the occasion . . . The rump of the grey horse in front of me must be almost four feet wide. And Cheyne's back isn't much narrower. He and Tiger would be a matched pair if the Tiger weren't about three sizes smaller. Both packed into their clothes. Bursting at the seams. And I see Cheyne's gelding's taking one step to Finisher's one and a half! What a monster! Cheyne never rides anything but greys. I've heard him roaring about his theory on it: 'A grey's either a very good hunter or a very poor hunter. I know where I am with grey!'

He knows where he is with grey!

His horses are like him. Nothing stops them. When

other riders are ducking and diving around the place, everything confusion and people wondering what's going on, you see Cheyne looming up at a slow canter with a loose rein, aimed straight at some huge obstacle, a hedge on a bank or something like that, and without pausing or gathering himself or taking up the slack in his reins and without any change of expression or stride he goes up and over, twigs and branches and clods of earth exploding around him, and once over he keeps going at the same pace and disappears into the distance. Everyone standing around gaping, not a hope of following him. And that's the only view of Cheyne some people ever get. *They* might imagine he's a romantic figure. He's not. He's hard. Few claimants for deer damage compensation would have the courage to dispute his assessment of their due, and none would have any success in altering it. He makes no secret of his contempt for people who, for one reason or another, might need to take things a little carefully. Morris's wife has no reason to love him. When she reported to him that her mother and father's vegetable garden, up in that dump behind Monksilver, had been eaten out by a herd of hinds in one night last winter he refused to go over there and assess the damage, or even to explain *why* he wouldn't go. The thing with Cheyne is, he's not a tenant farmer like the Tiger. He owns a freehold estate of over twelve hundred acres and his four sons and their families work it for him. He used to be a rugby international and, though some people might wonder about this, he's an educated man. Really he's in another class altogether to the Tiger, an enviable position somewhere between the responsibilities of the old gentry and the dependence of people like Tiger himself, but he doesn't let that get in the way of his friendship for him. Cheyne's a squire! And in some ways Tiger's probably about the only man he really respects. As an equal, or near-equal. Of course that's not down there in the valley crutching sheep and feeding pigs, or sitting around in Roly-Poly's parlour. It's a respect that only operates up here. On the hunting field.

But, after all, it's not just Cheyne's peculiar way of taking obstacles in his stride, or the fact that he is like him, though larger, in his temperament, that has cornered the Tiger's admiration. They might be friends without these things; what makes Cheyne special, what marks him out even among the few around here who know what deer-hunting's really all about, is his almost uncanny ability to be in at the kill after the most bewildering runs when hind-hunting during the winter. Hinds are light, they are thinkers, and they can run for ever. They are native to the iron winter, it being in their biology, and any one of them looks much the same as another, especially when momentarily glimpsed through a sheet of freezing rain. They can change ten times a day, putting the exhausted and bemused hounds on to fresh quarry every half-hour or so if the huntsman is not alert. Elusive is not the word for them! There must be times when even Jack Perry has come to a standstill, alone and out of luck in the dark at the end of a fruitless day, and wondered whether he was hunting a hind or some kind of trick of his own imagination.

Being there when one of these wild females is finally run down and can run no more, takes other things than brute force and self-confidence. As well as luck, it takes knowledge of the moor and of the habits of the deer; and it takes a certain artfulness as well, a local, an almost inherited, *feel* for the business. But apart from all these things, which Tiger has as good a share of as anyone else, for a man of Cheyne's immense weight (probably seventeen or eighteen stone mounted), it also takes at least two very large, intelligent and well-fed horses; horses with massive size, heart, muscle, and stamina, a combination of qualities not arrived at by chance. Breeding, in other words. And Cheyne's got them. He can afford the best.

And that's where the Tiger gets left behind.

That's where not only Cheyne, but Mrs Grant, and Lord Harbringdon and Jack Perry and even Tolland leave the Tiger behind during the big gruelling runs. If the Tiger were nine or ten stone there would be no problem. But he's fifteen stone and like Harry Cheyne he needs big horses. For horses there is a rule: the bigger they are the better bred they must be. Large ill-bred horses are the worst kind. They are death traps on this moor. I can pick out half a dozen from here, right now, lolloping and stumbling around the place, tripping over their own feet and getting in everyone's way. They won't be going far. Their riders will take a peek over the first hill, probably not see a deer, then retire from the field for the rest of the day to the pub.

If he's to stay with the hounds to the end the Tiger needs a big blue-blooded aristocrat under him. He's never been able to afford a horse like that, and in the normal course of things never would have the chance to own such an animal. Then suddenly there it was! Falling into place with the record harvest more sweetly than he could ever have dared dream: Alsop staggering around the corner of the rick almost begging him to buy Kabara, the wonder horse!

From the cheerful way he's going on there in front of me with his friend Harry Cheyne no one would suspect the Tiger of being at a delicate point in negotiating the price of this horse.

Twisting around in his saddle and yelling at me. Something about close up and stay with him. And here we go. Horses and cars and people and dogs all struggling and yelling and mixed up, a bottleneck as we turn into the pub yard. And there's Morris's car. No sign of Morris or Alsop but Mrs is sitting in the front seat waving at me. We're pouring through the gate and in to the stone-flagged courtyard, people all over the place trying to get a look at the hounds and Tiger and Cheyne roaring for a passage through.

Jack Perry's off his horse. He opens a low door in the end of a cowshed and urges the hounds into the dark hole. They don't like it, but the whips start singing and Perry has his way. The last of them in, he bolts the door. They howl mournfully for their freedom. We're all watching the huntsman. He eases the girth on his mare and things go quiet suddenly in the yard. There's a labourer staring at me, or staring, rather, at a point half-way down Kabara, his hands held loosely behind him, shoulders down, waiting and watching, without having anything to do. He looks away as I look at him and kicks at the wall with the heel of his boot, dislodging a silvery flurry of lichen from the old stone. I climb down off Kabara and lead him over near the Tiger.

Mrs Grant has joined him and Cheyne and they're talking animatedly about the condition of the hounds. The foot people begin drifting out of the yard, realising the excitement's over for the time being. Tolland and the second-horsemen go off somewhere, taking Jack Perry's mare with them, and the huntsman sits on an old mounting block and takes off his cap. There's a deep red line across his forehead and above that, in contrast to his weathered face, his skull is white and shiny. He gives his head a vigorous rub with the palm of his hand before jamming the hard riding cap down on it again. He's waiting for John Grabbe, the harbourer, to bring in his report.

I loosen Kabara's girth and lean back against the sunlit wall. My thighs are throbbing pleasantly from all the riding. I feel good. Hungry. It's warm, and I half listen to Cheyne and Mrs Grant and the Tiger talking, without actually following their conversation. They'll go round to the front of the pub in a minute or two and have a glass of sherry or brandy, or whatever it is they drink at this time of day. They're staying mounted for that. Out through the courtyard gate I can see the people and riders milling around, and cars nosing their way cautiously down the street between them, hoping to find somewhere to park. Every now and then someone comes and stands in the gateway and looks around the yard expectantly, then, seeing nothing happening, goes away again. And after a few minutes I spot John Grabbe making his way through the throng out there. Few of them know who he is, or that it is *he* we are waiting for—the master, the huntsman, the hounds yelling again now in their black hole as if they have winded him. And even impatient men such as Harry Cheyne and Tiger Westall—they all wait for John Grabbe on these mornings without complaining. He's riding to this meeting place mounted on a damp-looking mud-spattered moorland pony that is half asleep. He's been out slotting deer in the dark most of the night, or at least since the worst of the storm passed. There's a scruffy-looking spotted scarf pinned at his throat, almost as if he must intend a private joke by it. That it could be taken to represent a silk hunting stock, perhaps. His jacket's open, and under it he's wearing a dirty grey woollen jumper over a black waistcoat, and under that a few more layers of clothing. His pony's coming along head down, plodding, going by instinct, smell or something, habit maybe, but not by eyesight because its eyes are closed! He makes his way through the last of the sightseers on the road, overhearing rumours and speculations about stags seen in the area lately, but not looking around or saying hullo to anyone. Knowing all and saying nothing, he rides into the yard. The minute Cheyne and Mrs Grant and the Tiger see him they stop talking and turn their horses and watch him with great interest, but they don't go over to him or call out. Jack Perry gives his hat another firm push and stands up, going forward only the last couple of yards to meet the harbourer and putting his hand on the pony's bridle; 'Good morning, John. What have you got for us?'

The crucial question!

The huntsman's voice carries clearly across the court-yard, and the three enthusiasts here can't help leaning forward and rising a little in their stirrups, straining to catch Grabbe's response. The Tiger and his friends would love to get close enough to those two to tune in on this conversation, but both men have lowered their voices and are standing close together. You can see by the way they arrange themselves that their conversation is to be a private one. Grabbe dismounts, leaving the reins slung loosely over his arm, and he gets out his tobacco and makes himself a cigarette, his back firmly towards us. Jack Perry watches his every move closely, bent a little forward so as not to miss anything, frowning and nodding his head every second or two, his concentrated gaze following Grabbe's gestures as if the harbourer is about to conjure a stag out of the air for him. But Perry's expression lets us in on nothing definite, one way or the other, about the quality of the information he's getting. He shows no elation or disappointment. He's pressing Grabbe, he's prying and probing and cross-examining him, to get the detail out of him that he wants. And Grabbe shrugs and puffs his cigarette, he points up then he points down, mesmerising the huntsman with hints and possibilities, and once he laughs suddenly and takes a kick at a stone. It's all the same to him. He never hunts.

Sensing that something's up, a few of the more alert riders and foot people have begun gathering just inside the entrance to the courtyard. I see Morris and Fred Alsop among them. Alsop raises his hand to me in a nervous greeting, at the same time nudging Morris, obviously wanting to get him to come over here. But Morris stays planted where he is. Tolland has come up too, and makes his way through with difficulty, riding his own horse and leading Kit.

A moment later Perry signals Tolland to bring the mare over to him. The conversation's finished. He can get no more out of Grabbe. He climbs into his saddle and he and the whipper-in trot out of the yard together, the crowd at the gate parting to let them through, then closing behind them and trailing after them. They've gone to interpret Grabbe's news to the master.

This is not just a matter of being polite to the woman who's paying for it all; she mightn't have ridden a horse for more than twenty years, but Mrs Allen still controls the hunt. If they could get away with it, Perry and his hounds would chase almost any huntable stag they could rouse from the covers this morning. They want to get out there and get on with it. But she will insist that the stag to be hunted today is the most suitable, that it is the oldest stag har- boured in the area. And as far as she's concerned they can spend the whole day looking for that one rather than settle for something less. So now she wants a description from Perry of his intended quarry, a detailed description if she can get one, if Grabbe's actually *seen* the beast and hasn't just followed its footprints, though there's not much Grabbe can't tell about a deer from having seen its slots. She'll want to be able to recognise the animal that her hounds are chasing when she sees it, and should they happen to kill something else at the end of the day, Perry will have her to answer to.

Almost before Perry and Tolland are out of the yard Cheyne spurs his horse forward and calls, 'What's the news then, John?' And the rest of us, the Tiger and Mrs Grant from one direction, and Fred Alsop and Morris from another, with me and Kabara bringing up the rear, we all move in to hear what the harbourer's got to say. You can see he'd rather not hang around, but he has to wait here for Mrs Allen's decision, and then he'll take the huntsman and a few of the senior hounds out and show them exactly where the stag is bedded down. After that he can go home and get some breakfast. Or go out catching rats, which is the other thing he does for a living. Perhaps I should ask him for a solution to *my* problem.

We move in on Grabbe, as if *he* were our quarry. He's slow to respond to Cheyne, concentrating on nipping straggling threads of tobacco from a new smoke. He greets Morris and touches his hat to Mrs Grant. His skin is brown and shiny, drawn tight over the small sharp bones of his face, with scarcely a wrinkle in it, almost oriental. I don't know how old he is. At first he looks old, sixty or more, but the longer you look the more you see there's something young about him. About his eyes in particular, which are cheeky, or amused. As if he might be aware of a situation that no one else has noticed, and is waiting for the moment when someone *will* notice it, so that he may then share his amusement with them. His expression makes me want to look around, to see what the source of his amusement might be. To these hunting people he's a mystery man. A troll, out of the earth and bracken and forest. Smelling like a deer himself. He gets a meagre living from them, but he does his work alone, not sharing it, secretly. None of them really knows exactly how he goes about it. Perhaps he doesn't know how he goes about it himself, not in a way to tell anyone. Exercising an instinct for such things. A sense of how things are in the woods about him. The bending of a twig or the cropping of a leaf, staring signs, shouting events at him, and where others see only a confusion of muddy footprints, he sees the time and the place, the size and the direction, the age and the sex of the animals that made them. The detail of events accumulating in his awareness as he moves slowly through the grey dawn, or stands for an hour, still, receiving information in the dark. Attuned more finely to the ways of the animals, at last, than to the ways of humans. And doing all this while others sleep. People are bound to wonder about him.

It is said Grabbe lost his home and his family and his job as an estate manager years ago through this obsession with the forest and with the habits of the nocturnal deer. Roly-Poly would say he was drawn away, that he was seduced by his taste for it, like an alcoholic, or an insane person with a delusion, by degrees going deeper, until in the end he had abandoned everything useful, and was ravelled up and lost in affairs to which sensible people give no more than a passing nod. What can be got out of such entanglements? They are a disaster! And she would suspect him of touching on the power to curse or cure. One of *them*! The crazies! A threat! That's why she keeps well away from hunting. She sees too much of this kind of thing in it. Too much relying on insights that ordinary people know nothing about. Knowledge that can't be decently accounted for or explained. Relying on crazy freaks like John Grabbe to tell you what to do? That can't be right! And all of it going on up here, away from civilisation! Away from the work and the crops and the regular business that holds her life together. She doesn't come here, because she doesn't want to know about this consultation in the backyard of the Royal Oak at Winsford. She'd feel sick and scared if she had to witness the way her husband is so passionately interested now in the words of this ragged little misfit from the woods who's messed up his own life. And what about this trembling black fortune standing at my heels? What about this entire with the strange Australian name? Kabara? Why give a horse a name like that? What can it possibly mean? And it's on the point of soaking up half her harvest money! What about that? It would make her dizzy to see it all swimming together like this in the yard of the pub here; all the money, and the good health, the lives even, all hanging by threads, hanging by sudden accidents or by decisions made hot. Why risk all good things on this business?

Cheyne's voice booms out over our heads: 'Well, come on John! What's it to be?'

The harbourer is looking at Kabara while replying to Cheyne. And that private amusement in his eyes has spread to the rest of his face, to his lips. His voice is soft, relaxed, unhurried, his few words concealing more than they reveal. It's easy to hear that he's not interested in what he's saying or in the question that's been put to him. His mind is on something else. Despite Cheyne's aggressive energy, his authority, his almost threatening mounted bulk which he is thrusting forward now, he's not having much of an impact on the harbourer. Grabbe is more interested in Kabara's feet. He comes over and reaches down, bending towards Kabara's off-foreleg, preoccupied with this action when he says: 'A stag went into Burrow Wood this morning.'

The Tiger and Mrs Grant nod knowingly at each other, as if they had guessed as much already. And it *is* a confirmation of what they've been hoping for. Cheyne urges his mount in even closer, not satisfied with this, wanting more. Grabbe slides his hand down Kabara's foreleg and eases the foot up to inspect it. At this, Alsop and the Tiger check each other nervously. What's going on here? Grabbe gazes steadily at the underside of the hoof for a few seconds, everyone staring at him and waiting. Then he puts it down; Kabara is still and quiet while this man's hand is on him.

Cheyne's not going to *wait* for his answer, he's going to squash it out of Grabbe! His massive horse is almost on top of us! I can smell it! Towering and powerful and, like its master, restless. Reaching with its head and sawing and pulling at the bit, its weight shifting dangerously from one great muscled leg to another, eyes wide with anxiety, hating to be forced this close to Kabara, soapy froth beginning to whiten its grey neck where the reins are rubbing and slapping, and a continuous rumbling and gurgling going on in its guts.

Grabbe gets hit a couple of times with flecks of saliva as he straightens from examining the hoof. Cheyne's right over him, his knee actually nudging Grabbe's cap a bit askew. 'Yes John? *Well?* He went *in* did he?'

The harbourer looks up at him: 'He did Mr Cheyne. But I don't know whether he'll come out for you.'

The Tiger laughs sharply at this, almost a shout, staring hard all the while at Alsop, who'd be over here in a flash finding out what Grabbe's interest is in his horse, if it weren't for this other sweating charger that's threatening to trample me and the harbourer to death any second.

Cheyne doesn't laugh. He's not about to ease up on the pressure either. 'Jack Perry and his hounds will take care of getting him *out* for us, John,' he says, reefing on the reins and forcing his horse to stand close, side-on to Grabbe, effectively blocking his way.

'Did you get a look at his "head"?' Cheyne's pushing hard while he's got the chance. He wants to know as much as Perry knows. He wants to know it before things start happening, before Grabbe goes home to his breakfast and there's only rumours and speculations left to go on. He wants to be set up sweetly with the facts before the inevitable confusions and complications and the accidents of the run start to develop. He wants to be sure of what he's up to and to leave to chance as little as possible. He's after a decisive clue that will enable him to distinguish this stag from all other stags when he first sees it, and not be misled by false starts after the wrong deer, or become confused when this stag changes the hounds on to the line of another later on. He wants to be certain that he can remain staunch to the line of the original quarry when others have become unsure of it. You can see that he doesn't care if he's being rude. Annoying John Grabbe doesn't worry him in the least. He won't back off till he's squeezed as much information as he can out of the harbourer, and a description of the peculiarities of this Burrow Wood stag's antlers is what he's looking for from Grabbe, a definite identification. The stag's unmistakable signature. He believes this much is his due.

Grabbe turns to me, his palm resting lightly on Kabara's neck. 'They don't all have "heads" do they?' he says quietly, friendly, taking his time despite Cheyne's urgent pushing and shoving, speaking directly to me, almost as if he might even consider that there are no mysteries for *either* of us in this business.

But what does he mean? Can he mean he's seen Kabara's tracks at the soiling pit of the Tivington nott! That he's slotted us there? Is this what he's just been checking on? The print? *Kabara*'s signature? *Our* trace left there in the mud on the verge of that dark spring? Is that the connection he just confirmed for himself? Or am I jumping to a crazy conclusion? Is he telling me he knows all about the nott's new home and my visits there, or is he telling me something less than that? Should I just accept that he knows? My instincts urge me to. There's no way of being sure with someone like this. *Whatever* he says, he seems to suggest that he knows more and *means* more than he's actually telling.

Before I can say anything he turns away, ducking under the nose of Cheyne's horse and going over to where he's left his pony standing. I look up and meet Cheyne's aggressive gaze fixed on me. He's debating with himself whether or not it might be worth asking me what Grabbe has said. The minute I look at him, however, he decides against speaking to me, wheeling his horse aside and going after the harbourer. At this moment the intermittent dismal howling of the imprisoned hounds surges up into an excited chorus, and Grabbe kicks his pony into a trot, eluding Cheyne and crossing the yard to intercept Perry and Tolland, whom the pack has got wind of returning through the gate.

I'm hit by a gust of warm alcohol and tobacco breath close to my right ear. 'What did he say to you?' Alsop asks, sounding winded and anxious, getting to me ahead of the

Tiger. 'He didn't reckon there was something wrong with Kabara's feet, did he? Anyone would have to be pretty bloody stupid to think that!' He reaches down, leaning his weight heavily against Kabara's shoulder for support, and with difficulty he examines the underside of the stallion's hoof. 'Sound and clean!' he says, angry, as if he's proving a big point. He gives a groan as he straightens up, and puts his hand on his side, beginning slowly to knead his ribs with his long bony fingers. He's close, standing next to me. We both look at Kabara.

'What do you think of him?' he asks me, as if it occurs to him suddenly that my opinion might be of some interest. When I don't reply immediately he looks at me. His face is greyish and chalky, tiny dry flecks of skin lifting from his cheeks, and the flesh hanging loosely from the bones of his skull as if there is no resistance to its weight any longer in the muscles. Seeing me reading all this in his features seems to amuse him, and his eyes, at first weary and preoccupied, brighten up with interest. He smiles slowly and sounds more relaxed when he asks, 'Do you know much about horses?'

'Not much.'

The Tiger and Mrs Grant converge on us. And there's disappointed Harry Cheyne returning across the yard. Morris is hanging back from it all. I catch his eye and he makes a face of mock alarm. He's enjoying seeing me stuck in the thick of it. Tiger rides up close to me and he leans down from his saddle. 'What did Grabbe say to you, boy?'

Here they are! All of them! Surrounding me. Waiting for my answer to the big mystery. What do I make of it?

What will they make of it? There's nothing else to say. They are waiting.

'He said not all stags have heads.'

Mrs Grant turns to Cheyne as he comes up; 'Grabbe's harboured a nott for us, Harry.'

He reins in next to her and sits there, digesting this unexpected information, not looking particularly convinced. He scarcely more than glances my way. There's dislike or mistrust in this, maybe he hates to depend on an outsider for *anything*. I don't know. That could be my paranoia. He's checked in his quest for reliable facts, anyway, that much is certain. Mine is exactly the sort of information he doesn't want. It signals the beginning of uncertainty and rumour, and it can lead to confusion. He sits on his big horse and he thinks. Accepting nothing.

But if Cheyne's checked, the Tiger's relieved. He's cheered up no end now we seem to have avoided focusing on the sensitive subject of Kabara in front of everybody. 'So he said he'd found a nott in there did he?' he says to me.

'He didn't say a nott. He just said they don't all have heads.'

Cheyne snorts at this, convinced beyond any doubt now that my information is worthless, obviously concluding that I'm confused and don't even know that a nott is a stag without antlers.

The Tiger knows better than to make this mistake and he glares at me. 'What do you mean?'

'What about the horse?' Mrs Grant's voice, loud and clear and direct, a voice pinning down the attention of everyone within hearing of it, cuts through, her question startling the Tiger and ending, for the moment, interest in my uncertain report about the possible nature of the stag. Everyone looks at me and Kabara.

'What did the harbourer say to you about the horse's foot?' A calm, self-assured woman, sitting confidently on her fine hunter. She looks physically fit and well prepared for this business.

'He didn't say anything about the horse,' I reply.

The Tiger's looking anxiously from Kabara to Alsop to her, and back to Kabara again, as if he expects the stallion to be snatched away from him any second.

'He's a noble creature,' she says, studying the stallion, not really *that* interested in my reply after all; 'but I shouldn't care to hunt the moor on him.' She looks past us then, seeing something beyond Kabara that interests her more, and she rises in her stirrups and waves, moving off as she does so and calling; 'Jimmy! Hold up!' and away she goes, heading across the yard to intercept Lord Harbringdon, who looks like he's probably on his way to assist Perry and Tolland draft out a few selected hounds from the howling motley in the black hole.

'Well, there you are!' the Tiger says, jubilant, almost pouncing on Alsop. 'Not an Exmoor hunter!'

Alsop looks from Tiger to Harry Cheyne. He can scarcely be seeing any real friendliness in *either* of their faces—and he puts his hand on Kabara's neck, caressing the horse gently. 'She doesn't know my horse.'

'Peggy Grant knows horses,' Cheyne says in a hard tone; nothing to be argued with, making a statement of fact, local knowledge again, closing the subject. He's had enough of this. He wheels his big grey and rides off towards where they're getting the hounds out; 'You coming, Bill?'

The Tiger's quick to follow him. 'Get up, boy!' he says to me, hardly able to contain his delight at the way this little exchange has turned out.

I tighten the girth and mount up, but Alsop puts a restraining hand on my rein, preventing me from following the Tiger. 'Well?' he says, gazing up at me, belligerent maybe, or if not that then at least making a demand; 'Your mate Morris reckons you know something about horses. I asked you what you thought of this one?'

Morris is standing about ten yards off, maybe within hearing, and maybe just out of it, depending on the level of our voices, but not watching us and obviously not caring one way or the other about the outcome. He's keeping apart from it. That's his way. Being his own man when his time's his own. He's good at that. Now he's having his day off, that's all. He's on holiday. He's standing there on the cobbles, shaved and washed and well fed, and he's feeling this warm sun soaking its way through his jacket and into the muscles of his tired back. That's what he's doing. In a trance by the look of him, I'd say. He and Alsop have probably had a couple of drinks together in the pub before we got here. Come to think of it, that would be just the sort of thing Alsop would insist on after getting a lift in Morris's car. He'd feel he had to do something. I can hear him carrying on about it. Them going off then, and Morris's wife staying back, doing her knitting and sitting up the front of the car as always. In place.

For some reason, seeing Morris enjoying himself like

this, looking stronger and more relaxed than he has since the exhaustion that overtook him at the end of harvest, makes me decide to tell Alsop the truth. Straight out. Which, for my own reasons, is not something I particularly like to do. 'He's a pretty special horse, Mr Alsop.'

He keeps his eyes on me, his hand still holding the rein. 'Pretty special?' He waits for clarification.

'Well, I mean he's out of my class! He's got a fantastic potential!'

'Ah!' he exclaims, relieved, gratified! 'Thank you!' Then he becomes intent; 'Listen! Will you tell that to your boss? Would you mind doing that?'

Would I mind doing *that*? What a joke! It's just what I mean about coming straight out with the truth before considering the consequences. This injured old man doesn't want my *opinion* about his horse, he wants my help to sell him! I should have kept my mouth shut! Played dumb! Shrugged my shoulders and mumbled something incoherent. Acted the giggling yokel! Before I know where I am I've almost been snared into taking sides. I rip the reins out of his grip and spur Kabara forward; 'Tell him yourself!' Are all Australians such simpletons? He calls out something after me, but I don't hear what it is; an insult I think.

The huntsman has nearly finished assembling his draft of tufters by the time I get over there. There's John Grabbe, Tolland, Mrs Grant, Lord Harbringdon, the two second-horsemen, Cheyne and the Tiger, and they've formed themselves into a mounted semicircle in which the half-dozen or so liberated hounds are contained. Jack Perry is dismounted and standing in front of the half-door, about fifteen feet off it, the inert lash of his hunting-crop trailing on the ground in front of him like a black signature, the stock of this weapon held loosely in his right hand. He is confronted by a packed frame of clamouring dog faces at the opening. 'Bellman,' he calls softly, and, despite the noise, from down in the dim interior of this temporary prison, shuddering all over with excitement, the hound whose name has been called springs from his place, bounding forward and shouldering aside the younger ones up front; then, in a kind of private signal of gratitude, lightly brushing Perry's boots with his flank as he rushes past. For a second this great muscular hound stands still, gathering himself, then he goes half down on his stern and, tossing his black muzzle, he gives out a deep prolong-ed howl, his welcoming comrades in the draft nudging and circling and nosing him. Kabara shudders and stares down at this select group—most of them are the same dogs that had him up the bank half an hour ago—and he makes a threatening noise in his throat.

'Take it easy!' I plead with him, praying he's not going to start carrying on again.

Tiger pulls up alongside me, bumping his horse into us heavily in his hurry. Making sure that no one overhears him, while trying to seem off-hand about it, he says to me; 'Stick close today, boy. I shan't want that horse to be too fresh if Finisher gets done up.' And then he glares at me. 'You understand what I'm saying to you?'

I understand he'd like nothing better than to ride into Gaudon Manor after the hunt this evening and show Alsop a beaten Kabara. A horse unable to take the pace. Something like that. He's considering me narrowly. An odd sort of request for a master to make of his second-horseman. Will I do it without comment? My side of the bargain you might say.

'Well, boy?' he says, hating the fact that he can't just grind this out of me, but must actually seek my co-operation.

Perry's finished getting his draft of tufters together. Nine veteran hounds chosen to accomplish the trickiest part of the whole business. And now they're all wearing that slightly worried, responsible expression that hounds put on when they know they're the centre of attention. Every eye on Jack Perry shutting up the rest of the disappointed pack. Stuck in the hole! And that lot start howling and carrying on again the minute the door's bolted on them. Perry yells at them to shut up but they defy him and howl all the louder. He climbs on to his mare and calls over Tolland and the two second-horsemen for a private conference.

I become aware of a lot of movement and noise behind me, and I realise the yard has been filling with riders. They're pressing forward, eager to hear where Perry's going to draw for a deer. The two second-horsemen have been told something. They know more than we. They've had their brief word with Perry and they're heading off, forcing their way firmly through the crowd and out the gate. They know what's going on. Tolland raises his whip and yells for a passage through for the tufters. There's a fair amount of confusion developing as those behind keep pressing forward, while those in front turn into them and try to get out of Tolland's way. There's a flare-up of temper. Someone in there's had more than one sherry, for certain. Some of these people couldn't care less about doing this thing cautiously, a step at a time. Get out on the moor and gallop! That's what they want to do. Play cowboys! A few drinks under their belts and they're mad for action.

Cheyne looms up, thrusting himself between me and the Tiger and booming, 'He's going to draw Burrow Wood, Bill!'

This is headline news.

Tiger turns to me and says fiercely, 'Hunt with him, boy! Hunt with him!' making certain of his message. Making doubly certain that I don't dawdle around all day, second-horsing and saving this champion's wind for a late run.

Cheyne and the jostling press of excited horses and riders sweep him away from me momentarily, before I have a chance to react. Then, rising up out of the noise all round me, I hear the words 'Burrow Wood', going across the crowd and back again, going around the yard, repeated time and again like an echo of Cheyne's voice. Something released by him. Setting them in motion. Everybody telling everyone else. It could be a magical chant bursting out of them. Burrow Wood! Relief and excitement. They're surging and swaying in the confined area of the yard, trying to make for the gate now and calling to their friends out in the even more congested road.

Kabara's handling the crush well, other horses don't panic him, and it's not difficult to manoeuvre him into line behind Cheyne and the Tiger, who've been quick to join the tight flotilla going along with John Grabbe and Perry.

Things start moving in a minute and we're soon shepherding the tufters out through the gate.

The word has spread. Cars are starting up, backing out of their parking spots into the narrow street, impatient drivers leaning out of their windows, gesturing and calling for room. They want to go! Now! No mucking around! Get to a vantage point! Be there first! It's their right! They're going to lose something that belongs to them if we don't get out of their way and let them through! Horses shying and foot people laughing all round them.

Jostled in the crowd, Morris is suddenly in front of me.

'I'm really going hunting!' I shout at him, a rush of enthusiasm in me at the sight of him. He touches his cap and steps to one side, half mocking but half serious in his acknowledgement of me. As I am swept past him I turn to wave, but he is shoved in the back and stumbles and doesn't see me. I realise this is a privilege Morris would despise if it were for himself.

Ahead of me the tufters go forward. Upright on his blood-red stallion, distinguished by the slim black line of his coat, Lord Harbringdon is leading them into the thickest of the press of people. He has no need to wave his crop and threaten as Tolland is doing, for the crowd offers him a space in which to go forward. By his side, Mrs Grant seems to ride in the lee of his presence. Cheyne's second-horseman is waiting by the gate. Cheyne sends him off with the mob to the vantage ground of Winsford Hill, to wait there and, hopefully, to see in which direction the quarry eventually goes away; so that from there he can patiently plot an unhurried course of interception and deliver a fresh calm mount to his master when it is needed. He'd better!

But that's not for me. Today I'm not an attendant. Today I am going hunting!

I settle in behind them and listen to Cheyne telling the Tiger all about it—information he's badgered out of Grabbe or Tolland. The Haddon stag, he calls it; this one we're going out to look for now. Laid up in its lair, settled in for the day, drowsing somewhere deep in Burrow Wood. They hunted him one autumn day last year and he finally gave them the slip in the darkness of evening. Last seen looking back from the summit of Tarr Ball Hill in the fading light. Then vanished. Not a trace. Till Grabbe watches him going into the wood early this morning. A big six-year-old with a great spread of antlers.

The Tiger twists round in his saddle and squints meaningfully at me, not too unfriendly, when he gets this information. I shrug my shoulders and try to look innocent. It wasn't me who said anything about this one being a nott stag. That was Mrs Grant jumping to the wrong conclusion. No matter what I say now, however, no one will ever believe I didn't start that rumour. It fits me too well.

Cheyne's going on, recounting the arduous run this stag gave them last year, getting himself keyed up for another big one today. And the prospect is stirring the Tiger too. Is his mind still on buying and selling horses? I doubt it. He's got me tagging along quietly. I haven't asked any awkward questions in front of his friend. I'm doing his bidding as if it's nothing remarkable. As if, indeed, it might be because I have proved myself in the past to be incapable of doing it the orthodox way; unlike Cheyne's efficient second-horseman.

In other words, his plans are working out. I wonder if he thinks he's bought me off? So long as he gets Kabara I don't suppose he cares what he's done. But when he's home this evening and he's telling her all about his day in the hunting field, I bet he doesn't mention to Roly-Poly that he paid his second-horseman to go hunting a red stag on Exmoor today! An expensive privilege by anyone's reckoning. Such information would certainly convince her, if she needed any more convincing, that her foreboding of a catastrophe is justified; that I am working a spell on him, or some such thing, its equivalent. How *else* could a labourer's boy wangle it? For, in permitting it, it must surely seem to her, the Tiger was doing *our* bidding. An oppressive image for her, me riding this black entire on the moor today. Both of us foreigners! Both *therefore* against her.

We press on up the road for a couple of hundred yards, then Tolland leads us away from the crowd, down over a grassy bank by a path to the river. In mid-stream Kabara stops for a drink, his head going down and his lips flapping at the crinkling current, lightly brushing the smooth round stones, playing with it for a delicious moment before sucking the cold water in long deep gulps. I can feel the enjoyment of it going through him. We stand then, alone in the fast shallow current, when he's finished drinking, the water cascading from his lips, the others gone on ahead, and we gaze across the warm fields towards the woods, everything bright green and yellow and the water sparkling in the sunlight, remembering being alone on other occasions in places like this.

I canter him through the stream and up the far bank. The effortless power of his body! How he steps, strides, gathers himself then leaps! Calculated and balanced. So precise I imagine I hear his joints and muscles click into place. We clatter across the Withypool road, showering spray around us as we go, diving down again almost at once and two long strides carry us cleanly over Winn Brook; this lesser stream only a hundred yards from joining the river. And we're up with the tufters and their depleted escort of hunters.

They've paused. Grabbe's pointing something out to Perry, while Tolland and Harbringdon keep the hounds away to one side in a tight group. As I come up they move off again. Climbing away from the bed of the stream, we cross a long steepening field of stubble and soon reach the edge of Burrow Wood, which begins at the point where the hill has become too steep to work with a plough.

There is an old, neglected beech and hawthorn hedge at this boundary between wood and field, its bank broken down in several places, at each of which someone has made a rough attempt to close it with stakes and barbed wire.

Grabbe leads us up to one of these broken places and gets off his pony. With our attention on him he goes over and picks up a stone. There, in the soft place where the stone has acted as his marker, is the neat fresh hoofmark of a stag. Grabbe gazes down at this large slot and Perry leans over him and looks intently from his saddle, examining it for some moments, but not dismounting. Then the two men look at each other.

'That's him,' Perry says. Nothing else. No smiles. No thanks. And he turns to Tolland, who is holding the tufters together about fifteen yards away, an aroused and shivering bunch of hounds. 'Let's have them!'

They understand this and break from Tolland without waiting for his release, converging eagerly on the track of the stag, where they get stuck into their work, snuffling and whining, scouring the earth with their muzzles before turning from this spot as if they have all received the one signal. They are released, gone quickly, plunging in over the broken bank and away into the woods, one snagging himself on the wire in his eagerness and rolling over with a sharp yelp of pain. The echo of his cry bouncing off the close hill.

The hunt has begun.

Tolland at once canters off to the right, the flapping red tails of his coat disappearing a moment later around a jutting promontory of trees towards where Burrow Wood again joins Winn Brook, the first water if the stag should decide to go that way. Perry stays where he is, motionless, staring after his hounds into the dark summer foliage of the trees, as if he will decide to follow them when he has considered something sufficiently.

The rest of us spread out to take up positions at different points around the covert. I follow the Tiger and Cheyne, working our way up the northern slope of what must be part of Winsford Hill, though still many hundreds of feet from its summit. The Tiger stations me at the entrance to a wide path which drives deep into the woods. He leaves me here to watch while he and Cheyne ride further on, going up the steep hill and eventually out of my sight.

I'm on my own. Far down the hill to my right I can see the dab of pink of Perry's coat, stationary in the stubblefield.

I wonder what he's waiting for? In front of me the wide silent ride winds deep into the dark green and dun shadows of the ancient woods. I peer down this track, shaded and thick on either side with bracken and underbrush. A bird is calling repeatedly in there; a sharp short urgent sound, again and again. Then it stops and everything is silent and still around me.

Those great dogs are in there too, somewhere. They are intently unravelling the labyrinth of animal scents, some of them perhaps staying true to the peculiar signature of the Haddon stag, approaching his secret lair, working the complex line closer to him by the minute. Undoing the puzzle. Hunting by scent. Another dimension! A closed world to us. A remorseless business once that elusive thread has been picked up and carried to its source.

There's not a sound now. I look down the hill to my right again. Perry's still there. Then Kabara is alert, his ears pricked forward, a shifting of his weight on to his hind legs and a low sound in his windpipe. He's gazing straight ahead.

The ride is empty. I can't see a thing. Nothing moving anywhere. Kabara's sensed something in there, however. I trust his reactions. He's not just on edge. I'm tempted to go in and take a look. But then, deep in the woods, maybe a quarter of a mile or more away, there is the sound of a hound challenging. It's not the baying mournful howl of a lone staghound in full cry on a stricken quarry, or the confident song of a dozen dogs hitting a fresh line together. It's a short urgent warning, a mixture of aggression and fear, the challenge of an immediate confrontation. Unexpected. Something's leapt to its feet in front of a hound in there for certain, and Kabara must have picked that up a second before the sound of the challenge reached us.

From our position in the sunlit field we carefully examine the shadowed ways between the trees. There's not a movement to be seen. A few minutes drag by like this, and I'm beginning to get blurred vision and a crick in my neck, when something startles a pair of wood-pigeons from their perch in the high branches of a nearby elm, their wings clapping sharply three or four times in rapid succession as they fly away. And there! Something is moving along close to the ground on the other side of the earth bank, coming this way slowly. I raise myself in my stirrups until I can just make out the backs of a file of moorland sheep picking their way along on the other side of the hedge. When the leading ewe reaches the opening to the ride she stops and stares at us, wrinkling her nose. Then, unimpressed, she gives a bleat and leads her gang out on to the stubble, each one pausing in its turn to give us the once-over.

Sheep! I nudge Kabara and we move forward into the shade, the click and scrape of his steel shoes on the stones of the stubble-field muffled abruptly as we step on to the soft mulchy surface of the track. It's cool in here. There's a touch of the chill and dampness of the night lingering in the air, and the rich smell of leaf-mould and rotting vegetation. The smell of the earth. And what is it, then, that the *hounds* smell, travelling along so close to the ground? How *can* their 'nose' be sensitive enough to distinguish one deer's scent from another's while they're stretched at a full gallop, charging over the twisting criss-cross of conflicting animal scents? The pungent strength of what I'm smelling now must surely overwhelm a nose sensitive enough for that? But maybe, after all, it isn't like that, their sense of smell, but is more like our eyesight, picking up infinite shades of meaning, gradations of tone and intensity, not a single thread but a mosaic of impressions. The most acute hounds detecting, perhaps, traces that are scarcely present, no more than stale residues stimulating a memory of a scent, hinting at the passing, hours ago, of the hunted beast. Like that.

The best hounds enjoy working out their hunches. A matter of care and patience, of skill in deciphering elusive clues, disconnected possibilities dabbed here and there on isolated twigs and leaves. They keep at it and bridge the gaps, piecing fragments together into a coherent picture of events. But more than anything else, questing for the *right* deer when less persistent hounds have given up and changed to a stronger scent. It's these stayers that are prized by the huntsman, that are treated by him like a nobility. It's these rare hounds that I've heard Perry and Cheyne and some of the others refer to as 'staunch to a line'; solemn with respect while saying it, as if they were talking about a quality in those dogs that is a mystery even to them.

I sit still on Kabara, staring down at the debris: the roots, the leaves and the small plants, the twigs and the other odds and ends which make up the intricacy of the forest floor beyond the edge of the path, where it has remained undisturbed and has accumulated. I can't help feeling shut out from this place, finally, to think that so much of what is really here is beyond me, hidden from me, is in a dimension that I can't assess. It's no good kidding myself about that.

I let Kabara walk on further after a minute or two, along the track to the first bend. Here we stand, peering around the corner, deeper in to the shadowed recesses of these old woods. It is all still. If I didn't know the hounds were in there working feverishly at this minute I would think it all deserted too. There *are* sounds about me, if I consider them, small scrapes and clicks, twitches of the air in the foliage and amongst the litter of the ground, shiftings and scuttlings at the corners of my vision. But through it all there is a longer silence, of something withdrawn. The same silence I've detected before. Always the same. Maybe the hounds belong here, in a way, through being hunters to the bone, through their ancestry, or something like that, but Kabara and I are intruders. We'll always be intruders here, no matter what we do and no matter how long we stay. And if we *were* to stay I'm sure the forest would move away from us and establish itself elsewhere.

I wonder if John Grabbe feels like this? Or has *he* somehow managed to slip past? Has he gained a special access? That's the impression he gives me. That he's done something like that. But if he *has* done that, most people would say he's paid too dearly for the privilege; whatever *that* is! There'd even be some who'd claim that perhaps he's no longer really quite one of *us* because of it; and one of them would be Roly-Poly. The hunters need him, so they say nothing.

I become aware that I've been hearing, for maybe several seconds, way off in the distance, the outpouring sound of a number of hounds in hot pursuit. And at the moment I realise this, a hind comes into view, cantering along the ride towards us. She's not panicked, not fleeing madly or scrambling along, but is cantering evenly and with a purpose, swiftly but contained. We are stationary and she doesn't see us until Kabara shifts his head for a better look at her. She pulls up at once then and gives a short cough, staring at us, maybe thirty yards off, assessing the situation calmly. Even from here her gaze is relaxed and intelligent.

She is obviously in fine late-summer condition and, except for where a shaft of sunlight is showing up the rich russet of her coat, her colouring blends her almost perfectly into the background greens and browns of the covert. And if she were to remain stationary, even that bright patch of fox-red might confuse the eye and conceal her true shape. Her face is long and bony and her ears too large for her to seem pretty or fawn-like. Quite the opposite. Sitting here looking at her, I see she has the serious features of a calculating creature. At this time of the year she would almost certainly be suckling a calf. But there's no sign of one. It must be planted somewhere for safety, keeping still as a stone, its small body flattened against the earth deep in a great brake of gorse or bracken out on the moor, or through the other side of this wood on the farther flank of Winsford Hill, which they call the Punchbowl because of its shape. She stands there gazing at us for maybe three seconds. Then, without obviously gathering herself for it, startling Kabara with the suddenness of it, she springs upwards and sideways, effortlessly clearing the first dense thicket of scrub and bracken at the side of the track, and she lands soundlessly amongst the trees somewhere out of our line of sight.

I release Kabara and he jumps powerfully off his hind

legs straight into a gallop, almost leaving me behind. Sling-shot! We're at the spot from where she made her leap in seconds, but there's not a sign of her. Not a movement anywhere. She's gone! Vanished! Or is it possible she's squat-ting down in there? Standing stock-still, even, in full view, watching me? Waiting to see what I'll do? Waiting for me to make a move? To make a mistake? If I were to go scrambling around in there, penetrating the thickest of it in search of her, would she sneak out silently and head back the way she came, establishing a mile start on me, while I was blun-dering about taking minutes to get out of it and back onto her trail?

Someone's shouting at me. I look up. Galloping along the ride towards me on the track of the hind is Mrs Grant in desperate pursuit of three hounds, who are streaming ahead of her in line, looking just like the dogs at Catford Stadium chasing the electric hare on a Saturday night. She's waving her crop and yelling at me, 'Stop them! Stop them!'

I snatch at the reins and Kabara, startled out of his wits, snaps into a series of fancy pirouettes, spewing the brown humus around us in a shower. I hang on, only just, and call out, 'Stop! Stop!' – the world whirling past me while the hounds swerve round us, like a little volley of torpedoes, and head on up the track at seventy miles an hour.

Mrs Grant pounds past ten yards behind them, missing us by half an inch, and covering me in another shower of small clods. Maybe she mouths a silent remark at me, too, I think. Kabara dances around some more, lashing a wild kick or two at possible attackers, just in case there really are any, before more or less settling down again, quieting his amazing instinct for self-preservation; but still trembling, ready to go again now that I've managed to stir him up. We stare down the track after Mrs Grant and the hounds, in the direction of the stubble-field. They've gone. I was lucky I didn't come off Kabara then. And it's just as well the Tiger didn't witness my performance, it might have given him second thoughts. It was being alone that did it; seeing that hind so close caught me off guard. I got carried away. I forgot we weren't actually hunting *her*.

I hesitate, wondering whether to follow Mrs Grant and the hounds, or whether to hang around here in the woods and wait a bit longer until Kabara's thoroughly regained his calm, when the three hounds come bowling back around the corner. It must have taken them the best part of a hundred yards to realise they'd run out of scent. They're coming along towards me at a trot, no longer single file, but questing from side to side of the track, noses down, tails up, silent.

I'm not sure what I should say to them in order to stop them, so I yell, 'That'll do!' riding towards them and waving my right arm about. The yellow brindly-looking dog in the lead glances my way, then goes on with what he's doing. The other two don't even look up. Kabara is not enjoying this. He knows I'm unsure of what I'm up to, and he's ready to start deciding things for himself again any second. I give the wood-hard, muscular bow of his neck a reassuring pat and guardedly shout at the hounds, which are now making their way around me; 'Okay! I *said* that's enough!' I haven't got a whip or a crop, and I'm wondering if Kabara would stand for it if I were to break off a branch and start lashing at the dogs with it, when Mrs Grant canters into sight again.

'That was well done!' she shouts, sarcastic, driving her horse straight at the brindle hound as if she intends pulping him. 'Get out of it, Max!' Spurring her mount and holding it in at the same time, so that the horse seems to be on the point of trampling or striking at the terrified dog; but she's got the business under control, you can see that. Then, finished with brindle, she swerves and descends on the other two, running them down and almost putting her horse over the top of them. 'Crossbow!' she yells at the scuttling dog, and, 'Roger! Get on out of here, you damn fools!' She's all action! A remarkable sight here in the dark woods! Her black coat flapping and her beautiful expensive white buck-skins drumtight over her strong thighs! A horse-woman! The real thing. She gathers them up and herds the three hounds ahead of her, back the way they came, down the ride deeper into the woods, returning over the hind's scent but not hunting it now. And having set the dogs firmly on their way back to work, she hauls in her horse and she turns and takes a look at me. The once-over! Then she says, 'You *are* all right, I suppose?'

'All right?'

'You're managing that horse, are you?'

'Oh, him? Yes, we're okay.'

'Good,' she says, but I don't think she's convinced. She sits there considering us for a second or two longer making up her mind, then she says, 'Try not to get in the way.' And she canters away up the ride after the hounds.

We're alone again.

I want to yell after her; *I* know where the great Tivington nott is harboured! None of *you* lot know that! Like Cheyne,

she's decided I'm an idiot. It can't be helped. For one reason
or another it's always going to look like that to them.
No wonder John Grabbe doesn't hunt. Nor Morris. I walk
Kabara back slowly along the track and out on to the sunlit
stubble-field. We go through a cloud of dayflies, or whatever
they're called, gnats, tiny luminous things jiggling madly,
massed in the air just at the entrance. Kabara flicks his ears
and I take a swipe at them, but they swerve away from my
blow like a shoal of airborne fish. Millions of them! Out in
the bright field again, I look down the hill. Perry's still there.
In exactly the same position. The only other sign of life
about the place is someone standing way over behind him in
the shade of a solitary walnut tree. Whoever it is, they're not
exactly poised for action. While I'm watching, the figure
moves out into the half-sunlight and sits on an implement
that's parked there. It's probably Grabbe.

The heat is rising up off the glowing field now, a moist
smell of grain and wheat-straw rising with it, and the only
movement for the next half-hour or so is a little black and
white bird over near the ride. It darts out from a holly tree,
snatches something from just above the ground, checking
left and right at each dash, then flits back again into the
tree.

We're both watching this flycatcher when Kabara lifts
his head. This time he gazes up the hill to our left, in the
direction taken by the Tiger and Cheyne. It's a long way off
but, listening carefully, I just pick it up. Someone yelling.
A high, drawn-out cry repeated several times. It's a view.
Somewhere up in that direction they've seen the stag break
from the cover and gallop away. I can't hear any hounds.

I listen for a bit longer, but there's nothing more. Perry won't have caught that cry from where he is, so I suppose I ought to go down there at once and tell him. I hesitate for a second or two, then start down at a trot. I know how Mrs Grant or Harry Cheyne would be doing this. They'd be standing in their stirrups, galloping down the hill, yelling at the top of their voice and waving their hat.

I'll just tell him.

We're about thirty yards from him and I'm on the point of deciding it's time for me to speak up, when Tolland appears at a gap in the hedge, scrambling his horse over it and breaking out into the field. He canters up, calling out, 'He's gone away out over the Punchbowl. Half the field viewed him.'

Perry gives a grunt and nods in the direction of the trees in front of him; 'Half the field's not worth one of our hounds, though, is it, Mathew?'

We both look towards the point he's indicating, but there doesn't seem to be anything to see. Tolland says, 'I had it from Harry Cheyne himself.'

'And I have it from Bellman himself,' Perry replies drily, unmoved, offering no further explanation, gazing steadily into the woods. I look over towards the walnut tree. John Grabbe's still sitting on the roller, facing the other way, the pale blue smoke from his cigarette visible against the deep shade behind him. Tolland glances at me, then he trots away up the hill. Where's he going? I stay where I am, and a few minutes later we hear a hound opening on a fresh line. Unmistakable. This single voice is soon joined by another, and within a minute it's swelled into the ringing outcry of several voices. They're coming this way.

I hear a crunch in the stubble behind me and I turn round. Grabbe's there. He grins, friendly, and reins in next to me. 'They mean business this time,' he says quietly.

Perry looks round slowly at the sound of Grabbe's voice, 'He's never been far away.'

'Pushed his squire out ahead of him over the open country and turned back this way himself,' Grabbe says.

'Just the one?' Perry asks.

'I counted eighteen hinds going in there this morning, but there was only the two of *them*.'

'We can expect him,' Perry says, and neither of them speaks again. We watch the woods; the howling and yelling of the hounds getting closer. A grey heron screams and a pair of them rise slowly from their perch in the treetops, wheeling away sharply at the sight of us. And silently, here he is at the edge of his covert. He turns his head slowly to examine us and the branches of his antlers move like a fantastic headdress. Standing calmly, not a sign of fear in him. He turns again, listening to the racket in the woods behind him. We don't seem to interest him. The tufters are coming up fast on his fresh scent, but it's obvious he's made a decision about what he's going to do. He steps carefully over the wire, giving a hop with his hind legs, and he walks down the bank and out on to the stubble, standing now in the full sunlight. His thick shaggy coat is a rich red and the fine hard tips of his antlers are white. His eye is large and black and bold, his face flatter and wider than the hind's, and he looks at least twice her size. His gaze, passing from one to the other of us, passes over me and I see in him how he belongs to his own world. Wild!

With a light shake of his body, as if to rid himself of the last of his sleep, he moves off. With a lurching, easy canter he goes past us and down the hill towards Winn Brook, following almost the exact line taken by Tolland earlier, his pace so seemingly leisured that it makes me feel as though if I made a real effort I could catch him on foot. He's travelled less than a hundred yards when five clamouring hounds, with Bellman in the lead, scramble from the woods. Perry spurs his pony forward and intercepts them, cracking his whip and calling on each of them by name. When they come out of the wood, with their ears flattened by the wind and their sterns down, the dogs look to be travelling at twice the stag's speed, but they make up no ground on him. In fact he pulls away from them effortlessly. His action is genuinely deceptive; an unhurried long bounding movement really, which distances him swiftly, but which gives at the same time an impression of something a little ungainly. Watching him go away down the hill I see it is a hesitation in his stride, just at the instant he thrusts with his hind legs, a last half-chance to alter direction before the effort is fully committed. Perry has to lay in to a couple of his dogs before they're prepared to take him seriously. This close sight and hot scent of their quarry is maddening them and they hate to give up the chase! We watch the stag until he disappears around the promontory of trees. He's doing the opposite of what everyone perched up there on Winsford Hill was hoping he'd do, and many of them will go home today without having seen him. As far as they're concerned he may as well not exist.

The moment the stag rounds the trees and is out of our sight, Perry snatches his short hunting horn out of his coat and rips out a blast. Then, spurring Kit forward and urging the tufters ahead of him, without a glance at Grabbe or me, he gallops full pelt back across the stubble towards the village.

Shaken by the strange shrill blast of the horn so close to his ear, Kabara leaps in behind the huntsman and we're off whether I like it or not. I glance back at Grabbe. He's not moving. His job's done. But I've no time for waving. Kabara's tucked himself in close behind Perry's bounding mare and I'd better watch where we're going if I want to stay up. Perry drives at the hounds, his reins gathered tightly in his left hand and his right hand jamming the mouthpiece of the horn to his lips, blowing repeatedly a rising four-syllable note, rousing the countryside, announcing to all hunters that a warrantable stag has gone away out of his covert and has begun to run.

There's nothing sweet or musical in the sound the horn makes, but something mad. A sound filled with alarm. Putting us on edge. Startling our nerves. Kabara lunges and dances unevenly in his stride and snatches the bit angrily at each blast. It's getting us going, though! Giving our hearts a shot of something!

A bit out of control, we gallop in a tight fast formation across the stubble-field and plough straight through the brook as if it's not there, showering each other from head to foot with an explosion of silt-filled spray, the shrilling note of the horn jabbing out around us, penetrating the wooded combes and jarring awake everything in them. This frenzied blaring of the persistent horn striking aside the calm summer morning. Like someone having a fit. Neither the stallion nor I see the bank until it is nearly too late. We smash down the sudden slope into the water, Kabara driven almost to his knees by the shock of his landing, and throwing me on to his neck, but recovering at a stride and 'catching' me with the saddle he pounds strongly across the river, his nose inches from Kit's thrashing tail; one unlucky step on these smooth stones and here's a violent end to it already! We slam up the far bank and skid out on to the hard black surface of the road, my left stirrup swinging wildly, leaping after these hurtling tufters as if we intend to ride them down and destroy them, Perry still blowing his crazy horn full blast!

We pull up outside the pub, people converging on us from all directions. As if they're coming to gawk at an accident. Rushing at us. Staring. Scared of missing out on something vital. The riders among them worrying how they're going to make sure of getting into a good position in a few minutes when Perry lays the pack on the stag's scent— lose touch with what's happening now and they know they could be out of it for the rest of the day. May as well not have bothered to turn up in that case. And the horde are returning down the road from Winsford Hill too. Anxious cantering riders blocked by the cars! Shrieking kids dashing in and out everywhere, daring the situation. Anything might happen. Up the hill one minute, down again the next. And here come Tolland and Mrs Grant, pushing

through with the other tufters that went after the wrong
stag. Perry's not waiting for them. He's given Kit into
someone's hands and he's climbed on to a fresh hunter. He's
going straight for the yard and the howling black hole.

'Open it!' he orders, and three labourers nearly break
their necks trying to be the one to do the job for him. The
door swings open and here they come! Sixty eager hounds
rush out! Falling over each other and yelping and leaping
around the place. Fresh! Mad to go and get that stag!
Bringing in to the yard with them the stench of their confinement, hot and aggressive. Bristles stiff and erect along
their spines, they rush at the tufters, snapping and snarling
and sniffing and licking, thrusting their muzzles here and
there, urgent for a lingering taste of that magic scent! Perry's
maddening horn has told them a huntable stag has been
roused, has been seen, has almost been touched by their
privileged comrades! Now they can't wait to go! Their
freedom's only minutes away. Let's run and get him!

The tension's too much for one young horse. Before his
rider can grab the reins he drops his head and arches his
back and goes leaping and stiff-legging around the yard,
scattering people and dogs and horses in every direction,
miraculously stamping on no one. What a sight! The Wild
West! But the young woman on his back knows what she's
doing and doesn't even look like coming off him. She just
goes red in the face and tenses up.

Perry couldn't care less about all that stuff. *His* face is set
to what's ahead of him. He's blowing his horn again and
leading Mrs Allen's pack of hounds out to stick them on to
that stag's track. Nothing's going to stop him hunting the

beast now! And we're all falling in behind him. Forming up. Just as keen. It's a cavalcade. A procession. Show time. The people on foot feel like cheering us. You can see it. We're crusaders going out. Death and glory! It's written all over us. We're pressing and pushing and jostling and bumping each other and we don't care. We're enjoying it. We're getting close to each other. You can smell us. There's horses letting go all over the place; great for the rhubarb! We should be singing. Who knows a good song? And here's the woman on the buckjumper, her stirrup clashing against mine. She's happy now, delighted.

'You saw him go away, didn't you?' She has to shout to make me hear.

'He galloped down to Winn Brook in the sunlight, towards Withycombe.'

We both laugh.

'Wonderful!' she says, gazing, a flame in her eyes, seeing the leaping red stag in her imagination, until the tide of horses pushes us apart again, then waving. She's a local. *She's* only young, but I bet her people have been here for ever. A thousand years. *They* are all here. They've come out of the woodwork for the day. Out of the woodwork and the stonework of the old houses that are stuck away among the coverts and combes and the dark plantations of this place. Not tourists these people, but they're out in strength all the same. They're showing their strength! Putting on a show. It's *their* customs that have stuck Perry up front blowing that horn and dressed in his threadbare scarlet coat. This business belongs to them. And they've dressed up for it too. They're riding thousand-pound horses whether they can really afford to own them or not!

There's Cheyne and the Tiger! They're coming down the road, or trying to. Boxed in behind a mass of vehicles and riders. Tolland's found his place at the tail of the pack and he raises his cap, waving it and catching Cheyne's attention. He flags across in the direction of Winn Brook and Cheyne acknowledges the signal gratefully; he and the Tiger at once give up trying to force a passage through the crowd and turn down over the bank of the river. A few others pick up on what they're doing and follow them. We turn down over the bank ourselves, forced into a bottleneck, and we cross the river.

We are quiet now as we enter the stubble-field. This is it. Everyone subdued by the thought of having to really face up to it. We all know that the weaknesses of riders, as well as of horses and hounds, will be revealed before the day's out. It's inevitable. It's a gruelling business, chasing a mature stag to his death. People have broken their necks trying it. There's a rider waiting out there in the field. It's Lord Harbringdon.

As Perry leads the pack to cross the foil of the stag Harbringdon rides to intercept him. Maybe he knows something extra. It's quite possible. For there's Mrs Allen's car, silhouetted against the skyline, already stationed on the Withypool road, way up the hill the other side of Winn Brook! How did she get there? And that's Grabbe who's leaning there talking to her, his pony munching the grass on the verge a few feet away, looking rather relaxed from here. Not so much up there to see the stag away, as to watch Perry lay on the pack. I'll bet those field-glasses are doing their job. Scanning around. Not missing much. And she could still have a view of the quarry as well as of us from there. Who knows what she and Grabbe can see?

Harbringdon and Perry are having a consultation and we bunch up behind them, waiting. Some impatience starting to show in the ranks.

Jiggling and snorting and prancing around going on. The delay beginning to irritate some. Pushing and shoving too. Positioning, and certain people not as polite about it as they had been earlier. Nastiness coming out here and there. I see Mrs Grant giving a loud-mouthed tourist a fierce look. He'd better watch his manners, or she might hand him something more substantial; capable, I'd say, of swinging her steel stirrup into someone's teeth.

A few riders decide they've had enough of this and they begin heading off up the hill behind us. From what they're saying, they're apparently placing their bets on the stag doubling back this way later in the day; but maybe privately, too, they've realised they're not quite as keen as they thought they were for a run with these fresh hounds; saying nothing about that though.

And here we go. We're off again. Moving along after Perry; like impatient kids in a cinema queue. It looks as though we might be going down to the point of the trees. Harbringdon must have given a convincing reason for all this. Perry doing as he's told!

Kabara's close to a start. He's responding to the tension; munching his bit fiercely, tossing his head and not liking that martingale. A pity I hadn't slackened it off those couple of notches while I had the chance earlier, while the Tiger was out of the picture. It's too late now. I'm not getting off at this point. I might never get back on again! Kabara's Irish blood is heating up fast at the prospect of a big run. He's going to be a handful-and-a-half in a minute. There's a mighty surge of energy flowing through the springs and muscles of his powerful body, and he's not far from doing something spectacular. I hope I can stay with him when he goes. Whatever happens, it's not going to be *my* decision. I keep talking to him and trying to ease the situation along the best way I can, somehow convince him to wait for the signal. And hope it's not too long coming. But I see I'm not the only one round here who's unsure where he's going, or when. There goes the buckjumper, having another little fling.

There's nothing certain for anyone here about the outcome of today. Once we're away not even Jack Perry can predict the result, though he'll be doing his best to determine it. And there'll be plenty of bets riding on him *and* the Haddon stag. Which is one good reason why, though they're not coming with us, even those three labourers who were at the kennel door back there won't be able to settle to their work again until they've heard how this business has turned out. They'll be waiting to hear what gets decided. One way or the other.

Here's the Tiger, coming in alongside me. His face flushed, his fat hands a little too solid on the reins; the Tiger's all hard red muscle and veins sticking out. Sixty. Pumped up for action. Finisher's feeling his oats too and steps in stiffly, sideways, giving us a whinny of recognition, his neck lathered by the constant rubbing of the tight reins and saliva dripping freely from his lips. The Tiger pulls up to look at Kabara, who's started whistling through his nose, and he stares at him, risen a little in his saddle and wide-eyed, not examining the stallion critically, but gazing at him, holding Finisher forward of his shoulder then, after a minute, pulling back and turning his attention to me. 'How is he, boy?'

'Ready to go,' I say, letting out a nervous laugh. I'm fully occupied. Kabara's fuse is about to fizzle any second. I think I might have my teeth clenched.

'You're managing him?' Is he joking? Like anyone, the Tiger knows this is the moment when temperament is proved. And I suppose that's what he's come over to check on. But it's pretty obvious he's not really *seeing* Kabara, or me either for that matter. What's undoubtedly still mesmerising him, is what he spied back there in the brazen sunlight, next to the rick in Solomon's; the dangling dream. If he were seeing the real Kabara now, instead of that, he'd forget forever any ideas of hunting on him, and would be thankful for the reprieve from a suicidal notion. Just look at the way he's holding Finisher in! Binding the horse. Kabara would be in flames at that, up in the air and over backwards in a flash with that kind of pressure on him. It would be so quick the Tiger would never know what had happened to him. Crushed. Blackness. Sudden and complete. No purple stars either! It's compromise or it's nothing with a horse like this one. Give and take. But mostly it's give a little, then give a bit more, until you've *felt* your way through the crisis. A matter of finding a way with Kabara. He hasn't got a temperament to be mastered. Not even by the strongest hands.

'He's okay . . . I think,' I say, that nervous snigger slipping out again. If we don't go soon, however, Kabara's going to take off anyway. What a sight that'll be! Something else for Cheyne and Mrs Grant to remember me by. The fastest second-horseman in history! And a few other flighty ones might decide to bolt with us.

'Don't try anything clever,' the Tiger says, sounding quite concerned—for the horse I suppose.

'Okay, Boss. Nothing clever.'

'You're not to think you can follow Harry Cheyne.' He's worried about my good judgement in these matters.

'I promise.'

'If you want a pilot, pick someone steady who knows the ground. Charley White's the man for you to watch.'

'Right!' Who's Charley White?

'Whatever you do, don't foul the line! Keep your place and hunt!'

'Okay.' Why don't I tell him? Right now before it's too late? Why don't I just yell it at him?

He's the master. He should know.

There's a whimpering cry up ahead, then the whole pack opens strongly on the hot scent of the stag. The amazing sound of over sixty hounds all howling and yelling at the same time. A moment of confusion, with some going in the wrong direction, and we're off down the hill, crashing out over the poor hedge of the stubble-field and pouring over the steep decline beyond. It's a race to the rocks and the water below! A cavalry charge! Panic! Every man for himself! A solid pounding mass of riders hurtling after the dogs. We couldn't stop if we wanted to. Where's the enemy?

We hit the water in a compact body and lunge blindly for the other bank. There's some floundering and staggering going on among the rocks—someone down I think—but Perry and his hounds are cleanly away, the leaders up already and crossing the road just above Mrs Allen's car. She's in the perfect spot. Not another car in sight. It looks steep up there. The youngest hounds are stretching ahead, competing for the lead, their voices mad and out of control with the desire to go. Sorting themselves out.

Now that he's been released Kabara's moving well. He's watching his step, making intelligent decisions and picking a good line through the crowd of hazards. He side-steps, lunges and leaps and we make it through the water. A hundred yard steep upward pull and we cross the road, losing ground rapidly to the leading hounds, and we charge into a chest-high stand of bracken, picking a twisting sheep path. The stag must have flown over this stuff, hardly touching it. The dogs have disappeared. A riderless horse tries to overtake us, crashing dangerously alongside, eyes wild, straining and struggling up the hill, not seeing where he's going, then clipping Kabara's heel and going down with a terrific crash. As if he's been shot. Spewing up a shower of bracken chips and wet earth. But we're out of range. Going hard. Kabara taking the slope with great energy. Loving it. Putting his strength into this hill. Ducking and weaving around the sharp twists and turns of the meandering sheep track. I've no time to check on who they are, but there are other riders close by; intent, silent, working at this big hill, making hard for the rolling ground on top. The crying of the hounds has settled almost to a melody and I glimpse them every now and then appearing and disappearing through breaks in the stands of bracken, a snaking line of black and white going unchecked for the summit. The scent must be burning on this drying ground after last night's rain.

A cooler breeze in my face makes me look up, and we're coming over the steep flank at last and on to the top. Kabara's drawing breath in great gasps but showing no sign of slowing. We burst out of the last band of bracken and gallop on to the sure, firm going of the low windswept heather and whortleberry—hurtleberry! There's a dozen others with us and we charge for the skyline, as if we're obeying someone's orders, the wind rushing against us, the vast distant rolling hills of the upland moor coming into view. But at our feet, almost a canyon, between us and those remote heights, is the deep wooded valley of the Exe. And there they are! Perry's red coat! And ahead of him the trailing line of hounds. Flying down along a steep spur and singing and calling and blowing his horn; and the dizzy drop below theml There's no turning back now. Here we go. Death or glory!

Out on my left someone yells, a challenging call, or a warning to get out of the way, and a blood-red horse pounds through to the lead. No sign of hesitation there! It's Harbringdon going full tilt for the valley! What a sight! His rush draws us in behind him, giving us a lead we can't refuse. He's our leader and we're a mad tribe of wild savages galloping headlong down the narrow spur into the peaceful valley below! If we fall we'll roll forever!

I've never done *this* before.

We haul in and string out single file, as the backbone of the spur narrows, shelving off steeply each side, weathered here and there to the bare red rock. Far below us, Perry and the hounds have disappeared into the woods. A minute later and we crash down the last, almost vertical, incline with most of our mounts sitting down and slithering on their haunches, forelegs stuck out and propping. But not one of us gets off and leads by the reins. It must be the way we feel. Reckless. A band of outlaws. A raiding party from the hills! Leaping and sliding off the final steep bank, through an oak coppice that whips and lashes our faces, we plunge into the river. Straight across and out the other side on to a grassy flat, lunging through breast-high water. The lead pulls up.

What now? Where did Perry go? Not a sign of him or a sound of his dogs either.

The last dripping horse clambers out of the river and we all stand there listening, or trying to, the horses grunting and blowing and wheezing, shaking themselves and rattling the gear, too winded to stand still. We are uncertain. Have we come the wrong way? If it were up to *me* from here, I wouldn't know which way to go. But *they're* sorting something out. Harry Cheyne's agreed to head off downstream while Harbringdon and a few others take a look upstream, when Tolland trots into view through the trees, looking unconcerned, his mount considerably fresher than ours, despite the fact that he's somehow got here ahead of us. But where did he come from? He's after a couple of hounds that have cast down the water, he says, touching his cap to Harbringdon—no mockery in his acknowledgement—and trotting on, calling over his shoulder that Perry and the rest of the pack have cast up the water on a sure thing. Something about a huddle of startled sheep being spotted in that direction.

So that's the way we go. Trotting along single file again, by a riverside track through the dense thicket of trees. There must be nearly twenty of us altogether now, though not all from the original hilltop 'band'. Quite a few others came down the spur behind us. The Tiger was among them, and the girl on the buckjumper too. Mrs Grant, I noticed, was with us all the way. We're moving quickly, no one talking or wasting any time. We break out of the trees after a hundred yards or so and cross a grassy glade—the sort of hidden place I love to discover on my solitary explorations—flanked and protected by the hill on one side and by the river on the other, it is sunlit and secluded, entirely enclosed by these coppiced oaks. Normally it must be a little world of its own. But today I'm with this platoon of cavalry trooping through. Keep your heads down till we've gone. We may not be friendlies!

Kabara's ears jerk forward and there's the horn! The hounds begin to speak too. They must be on to him! It sounds like they're about half a mile ahead. We speed up, diving into the whippy oaks again, everyone watching out, getting into a fast canter, ducking and weaving along the narrow path. No chance of passing here. Though look at that! There goes Harry Cheyne, cutting off to the right on a diagonal, spurring his horse and crashing through the untracked coppice like a charging beast. And he's right too. He must have picked it early. There is only a thin band of scrub remaining between him and open ground in that direction. I can see the purplish grey of the hill ahead of him from here.

We stick with the track and emerge from the trees some distance behind him, scattering for the hill ourselves. But he's snatched the lead from Harbringdon. He takes an extremely steep line, further to the right than us. Then, having got up some way, he cuts back along the inside slope of the hill on the precarious thread of a sheep track, which heads in to the narrow neck of the combe above us. He's obviously hoping to make a short cut across to the first terrace on the farther spur, and so get on to the stag's foil that way. And sure enough, there's Perry on the skyline now, sitting down and fairly cantering up the steep incline, just going in to the terrace that Cheyne's making for! Cheyne's guessed it right, but will he get to it? He must negotiate the head of the combe first, round the sharp inside elbow of it, and from here that looks dangerously boulder-strewn and steeper than the roof of a house. One slip there and he'll be down here again! None of us tries to follow him. But if he makes it he'll be almost up with Perry. *If* he makes it! His voice floats down to us from the hill, urging that big grey horse along as he gets into the slippery angle of it. Moor sheep, tracking along single file, have bunched up as they reached the rocks and have poached the ground, creating a mud trap just this side of them. A horrible spot to be sitting on the back of a mettlesome horse! If that grey refuses there's no room for him to turn round and retreat from it. It's no wonder the Tiger said not to follow Harry Cheyne! He's out of my sight for several seconds. I can hear him swearing but I'm too busy riding the hill myself to keep watch.

As soon as I get the chance I glance over that way. And there he is! Clambering out just above the boulders. With sound turf, by the look of it, ahead of him all the way to the terrace on the farther spur. Almost a flat run to get there from where he is. And the rest of us still with a stiff head-on climb to reach that spot.

What a manoeuvre!

Struggling upward, it soon becomes obvious that this hill is more massive and imposing altogether than the one we crossed to get into the valley. Except where the ground has been broken by sheep, beneath the hooves of our mounts there's a secure footing, a springy turf of tough ground-grasses with, increasingly in dense tussocks as we get higher, the coarse purple-flowering flying bent again—that primitive species which the Tiger and I first encountered early this morning when we came over the hill above Wiveliscombe. The real Exmoor grass, now in its late summer finery. The higher slopes above us must be the first of those great rolling undulations of open country that we saw from the peak back there. As well as being more massive, the hill is deceptive too, being not a continuous even upward slope, but presenting us rather with a series of steep inclines that level off abruptly in to terraces, or saddles, so that as we breast the upper bulge of each, with nothing visible but the blue sky above us, we keep thinking we've reached the real summit, only to be confronted by yet another mass of hill towering above us.

After what must be several hundred feet of this, the sheer toil of it begins to dishearten even some of the strong ones. Finisher sticks with Kabara for a surprising distance, the

Tiger urging him to his best effort, no doubt measuring the gelding against this splendid stallion, but finally being forced to drop back, sobbing for breath. He's not on his own in that. A good deal more than half the field are knocked out by this gruelling stretch and they drop out one by one along the length of the hill, forming a scattering—like the remnants of a defeated army—toiling up the slope. Many riders get off and attempt to lead their mounts, but soon find that the smooth leather soles of their riding boots, giving no grip at all against the steep grassy slope, make leading a nearly impossible task. Some of them stop, no doubt wondering if there isn't an easier way of doing it, or maybe even thinking about giving up altogether. Looking back I can see the Tiger. Not much chance of *him* getting off. He's standing in his stirrups, leaning forward over the neck of Finisher, one hand gripping the thick mane, the horse lurching doggedly upward. He stops for a breather as he reaches a terrace. The Tiger will do it by good management.

Ahead of me I can't actually *see* anyone. Though, apart from Perry and the hounds, I know Cheyne and Harbringdon, are up there somewhere. And I think Mrs Grant and one or two others might have got an early break on me, while I was preoccupied waiting for Harry Cheyne and his grey horse to fall off the rocks. Kabara's reduced to a rolling, lunging stagger by the time we come over the final crest, gasping for his air but not thinking of giving up, laying back his ears instead and snorting with an aggressive desire to get the hill behind him.

One minute we're still struggling up this seemingly endless series of hills, and the next we're there. Out on the open upland, the landscape dropping away from us in gentle undulations, falling, then rising and falling again as far as the eye can see. I've never approached the moor in this way before and for a moment I forget the hunt, gazing over this wonderful sudden prospect. Kabara's chest is heaving and he is content to stand.

Way past the high distant cairn on Dunkery Beacon, even beyond the moor and across the Bristol Channel, I can make out the coast of Wales. And beyond that, a final backdrop, the remote dark shapes of the Black Mountains of Glamorgan, grey shadows through this summer haze, mysterious and foreign. No way of getting there from here. I wonder what's there? I wouldn't mind going some day. Across the water. Just to have a look. There is a cool north-westerly breeze blowing steadily into our faces. I can smell the Atlantic.

Kabara is extremely fit and recovers his wind within a minute. He begins to look around at once for more action. Restless. Distracting me from my day-dreaming. *He* hasn't forgotten we're hunting, nor the other horses ahead of him. I get the feeling he doesn't much like the idea of that red stallion being out there. He wants to go.

But which way?

There's not a living soul in sight. Where are they all? They've vanished. The vast sweep of wild moorland before us is still and empty and silent. Not a thing. Not even a tree or a house or a road breaking the natural undulations of the hills. No startled birds flying up. Nothing obvious. They can't possibly have run to the horizon in that time. They must be hidden from our sight, down in one of the draining chines which I know cleave off in all directions from this top country. These heights have deceived me before into thinking I could ride straight across from one peak to another, only to find between them a deep wooded cleft snaking down to the valley below and barring my way. The moor is riddled with such puzzling seams, hidden, difficult places, where the gentle gradients of the open high country fall away abruptly into deep water-worn and thickly wooded combes, scrub and rocks in places, making them inaccessible to horses. The hunt could be entangled in any one of them by now. But which one?

We move forward at a trot. I hold Kabara in and look for a clue as to which way they might have gone. We travel almost half a mile, descending the slope into a great bowl-shaped arena between two rounded peaks. I am permitting the lines of the landscape to lead me, instead of thinking about what I'm doing. I'm just changing direction, turning towards the western ridge, when I hear them. Kabara too. And a moment later a dozen or so hounds come flying over the horizon straight for us. By the noise they're making they must be on a hot scent.

We pull up and watch them. Their line is almost straight; if they hold to it they'll pass within a few yards of us. They're running single file and clamouring as if their quarry is only inches from their noses. But there's not a deer in sight. The line begins to carry them more off to the right and they eventually go past us about fifty yards away, heading towards the eastern ridge. I've no idea whether they're hunting the right deer or not. There's not a sign of the rest of the pack, nor any riders, and this break-away lot could be after anything. With the scent holding as well as it is, maybe I should have tried to stop them and have waited for someone else to come up?

If I give Kabara his head over this good going, he might just be able to get in front of them even yet, before they reach the ridge and disappear over the edge into the valley. There'll be no catching them once they get that far. But if I'm going to do it, I'd better do it now. I release him. He knows exactly what's expected of him and gives it everything, needing no direction from me as to the right heading. He's on a line to intercept them at a full-stretch gallop in three or four strides, his hooves drumming evenly on the sound turf.

But those dogs are going faster than I thought they were. After less than a hundred yards I can see that we haven't got a chance of overhauling them. They reach the edge of the hill well in front of us and pour over nose to tail, slipping along at high speed.

I rein in at the lip of the slope and watch them running away from us, down towards the base of the valley. I still can't see what they're hunting. But the side of the hill below us here is thickly patched with interconnected brakes of high bracken and gorse. Anything could be hidden there. It's not an inhabited valley this one. There are no signs of cultivation down there. It is a minor offshoot from the Exe, rising upward gradually until it eventually joins the slopes of the high moor two or three miles farther on. Steep-sided here, narrow, rough sheep country, never broken by the plough, the only mark of civilisation on this valley is the tawny track of an unsealed road snaking along beside a rocky stream; itself a tributary, no doubt, to the Exe, curving around the base of this hill and joining the main river lower down, not far from where we crossed earlier.

There are several riders and three cars on the road. I watch them making their way slowly upstream. They pause then move on, as if they might be observing someone's, or something's, slow progress on the slopes above them. When I return my attention to the hill I've lost sight of the hounds. Searching the open patches between the bracken for them, however, I catch sight of their quarry! Seven or eight hinds are galloping along about two-thirds of the way down the slope, now wheeling sharply towards the cover of a tangled scrub where the foot of a rocky combe opens out, probably deflected from crossing the valley by the sight of the riders and cars below them.

A moment after the deer disappear into the scrub, I see what it is that the people on the road have been watching. A rider in a red coat emerges from the shadow of a couple of pine trees and moves down on to the line of the deer.

There's no doubt it's Tolland.

He must have left the river soon after we saw him, and turned up this tributary, following it around the base of the disheartening hill that finished off so many of the field. But is his presence down there now—so exactly positioned in the path of these break-away hounds—a happy accident for him? Or did he expect them? An uncanny prediction if he did. He moves out in to the bracken and raises his arm. A few seconds later the faint crack of his whip reaches me. He's stopped the hounds. There's a flash of white here and there as they mill around in front of him, frustrated. And now the distant sound of his voice berating them. And he's done it with little effort, not even getting his hunter into a trot!

The whipper-in. Doing his job.

Outrider to the huntsman. He's been doing it for ten years, and he has his own following. They are bunched up on the road below him, stationary, watching him bringing the wayward hounds down. The sound of their voices floating up to me out of the valley, thinly on the warm rising currents of air. He picks his way down the hill towards them, as if he has all the time in the world, and chases the dogs out on to the road to meet another couple and a half that have been in the safekeeping of one of the riders; no doubt the strays he was after earlier when we met him by the river. He'll be the huntsman one day. When Jack Perry retires or dies. A local tenant farmer's son; I've heard Morris say he was born within hearing of the kennels in Exford, and knows this country better than most people know their own kitchens, that he can travel about it in the dark almost as well as John Grabbe. He pauses now by one of the cars, then gathers the hounds around him and canters up the road with them, the others following.

I watch them for a moment. They must expect to intercept the line of the hunted stag that way sooner or later.

I could ride down and follow them, but it would mean losing too much hard-won height. And anyway, it would put me well in the rear. I'm not certain of the country in front of me, but it looks as though if I continue on in a north-westerly direction, sticking more or less to this ridge, I should be able to connect up with the head of their valley in a few miles. They've disappeared around a bend now and the road below me is deserted again. I can't see any sign of those hinds either. Not a shiver of movement in the scrub.

I turn Kabara's head and we canter into the arena again, crossing it and heading up the farther rise. He's glad to be on the move. As we come out over the top there are a dozen or more riders ahead of us, strung out and going on at a fast pace, maybe a mile from here to the tail of them. Taking them to be the leaders, I'm surprised to see quite so many.

Kabara lengthens his stride eagerly the minute he catches sight of them and we begin to close the gap. The going's perfect; gently undulating and sound underfoot; turf and increasingly extensive patches of tough short heather, with views to distant horizons in every direction. The cool air rushing past and Kabara moving easily, well within himself. We cover the ground rapidly.

This great confident horse under me!

When he sees how well he's going the Tiger will be wanting him soon enough. But for the moment it's me hurtling along, only the blue sky above us, hooves brushing the yielding heather. I shout his name and his left ear flicks back. He's happy! Energy! Driving hard across the landscape! Bred for this.

Before we overtake the tail-enders I begin to suspect that these riders aren't the leaders, but have come up the hill behind me and gone on ahead while I was mucking around chasing those hounds and watching Tolland doing his job.

A few minutes later, sure enough, I catch sight of the Tiger's squat frame bouncing along in front of us, his wide bum in those pale twill breeches like a big signal going on and off. I ride up beside him and slow Kabara to his pace, holding alongside.

It's a few strides before he glances across at us. He grins then, not looking surprised to see me and, without speaking, he points ahead, indicating the distant slopes of Dunkery Beacon, towards which we are riding and which rise above the level of this central plateau. It takes me a few moments before I make them out; a line of riders, half a dozen at the most, cantering along the side of the great hill, at least three miles ahead of us. The ones I should be with now if only I'd gone straight on. They're flying!

'Do you see him?' the Tiger yells, pointing beyond the direction of the riders, farther to the right, to the eastern horizon. I look, and there he is! Distant but unmistakable. The Haddon stag. Standing stationary on the skyline, observing his pursuers. Calmly watching them coming on behind him, almost as if he's waiting for them. I take my eyes off him for no more than a second, a quick check of the hill for Perry and the hounds, and when I look back he's gone. Nor any sign of Perry or the hounds either.

'I saw him!'

'He'll have gone down into Horner Water if Perry hasn't beaten him to it and turned him back,' the Tiger says, sounding pessimistic. And a minute later he adds, 'Could be the last we'll see of him.'

Kabara's impatient to get ahead. He wants to be up there with those leaders. He keeps twitching his ears at me, semaphore signals telling me it's time to stop slouching around back here with this tame stuff. But I coax him into holding down to the Tiger's even canter, and he grudgingly puts up with it. Both horses pound along side by side, blowing and grunting at each stride. Finisher is content to enjoy the open run, not looking for anything more demanding; Kabara is tossing his head every few strides —still annoyed by that over-adjusted martingale—and inclined to gather and lunge, looking for a break.

The Tiger'll tell me any minute to stay with him from here on and to change mounts at the first opportunity. And that'll be the end of my hunting career. I'm waiting for it. But he says nothing. And we go on together for a quarter of an hour or more, matching stride for stride over the heather. But this poking along easily is not Kabara's natural way of doing things, and being forced to hold to it for so long begins to put him off balance. I'll let him go in a minute. For the moment there's something in riding along like this—it will never happen again! The Tiger and I hunting together! And who knows, maybe *he's* even enjoying that side of it? Could he be feeling companionable?

If only Roly-Poly could see us now!

We're coming on to the side of Dunkery when Tolland appears in front of us, cantering up out of the head of the valley, tailed by his silent hounds and his small band of breathless followers. As soon as he gets on to the level, he turns in to the hill, his hunter giving a mighty leap as he does so; though from here there doesn't seem to be anything worth jumping.

We're heading to cross the road fifty yards behind Tolland, but it's not until we're right on the stony surface, at the very last second, that I see the deeply eroded drainage ditch on the far side! I tense up for the inevitable crash but

Kabara gives a snort of fear and leaps it without adjusting his stride. A magnificent reflex action! Like a wild animal! Almost leaving me hanging in the air. Finisher goes up and over easily a stride behind us, well under control.

I look across at the Tiger in amazement, my nerves standing on end, gooseflesh down my legs. How we flew through the air. The gaping hole going by yards beneath. Red pinnacles of eroded rock. The grand canyon of Exmoor! An aerial survey. Every grainy detail of it.

The Tiger nods, his expression guarded, clearly impressed by my survival. So am I! Overwhelmed!

I ride on a way—in a bit of a daze—before the nasty truth of this business begins seeping through to me. The way he took it, the Tiger must have known that ditch was there. Hasn't he hunted this country a hundred times? If he knew, why didn't he say something? Yell out a warning to me in case Kabara missed it? Instead of pulling back half a stride and watching us go into it blind? Which, looking back, is just what he did. Observed us! I've got a persistent after-image of him doing it: out the corner of my left eye, easing down a fraction and steadying Finisher, then falling away that half stride just before we hit the gravel. I feel a mixture of anger and embarrassment, my cheeks becoming flushed. Sitting back waiting for us to smash into that hazard full tilt! I'd call it a death trap! Saying nothing and riding along with me as if we were companions. I was on the verge of enjoying his company and all that time he was planning to chance my neck just for the opportunity of putting this stallion through one more test.

I've underestimated him again!

He's alongside. I can *feel* him staring at me, waiting. I wouldn't know what to say to him. When I finally glance at him he tries a wink and a smile; man-to-man stuff. But it's too late for that sort of rubbish. He's guilty. It was that guarded look I got from him when we alighted safely on the sound turf. I saw it. I *know* I'm right.

I touch Kabara with my heels and give him his head. He jumps forward, leaving Finisher for dead. Our move takes the Tiger by surprise and we make a good twenty yards on him before I hear him yelling some command at me. That's better. No winking or smiling in that. *That's* the voice of the Tiger! Irate. Do this! Do that! The roar of the *master*!

I'm back to reality.

I'll pretend I've gone deaf. Let him yell his head off.

Kabara's picking up his rhythm nicely, responding to this liberation and to my anger, striking out powerfully after Tolland's group. A *companionable* Tiger! What an imbecile to have indulged the thought! If Kabara weren't so brilliant the drain could have been the end of me. Just like Alsop and the wall. Another pushy foreigner struck down. Out of his place and he gets chopped. See that? Smash! Down he went. Never the same again. And back there in the Black Valley, stringing beans in her whitewashed kitchen, I'll bet Roly-Poly felt a twitch in her bones too, paused and looked up for a moment; wondering, hoping. Might almost have had me and Kabara out of the way in one hit there. She's been waiting a long time for something like that ditch.

Too bad.

I encourage Kabara to his best pace; leaning forward in the saddle and whispering his name into his left ear. We're too quick for *them*! If the Tiger wants to ride this stallion today he'll have to catch us. Let's see him do that on Finisher. Kabara's really moving now, his ears working backwards and forwards, light as a startled cat, seeing every blade of grass, scarcely touching the springs of the tough swaled heather, flying; his rich Irish blood on red alert. Racing across this foreign moorland! Even if I wanted to, I don't think I could pull him up and make him wait for the Tiger. I'm not horseman enough for that. He's got the bit in his teeth and has probably forgotten I'm on his back. He's a black savage with a hunting mind of his own!

If I survive this I'll get the sack for it.

Within minutes we charge up on Tolland's followers, scattering them and ploughing through. A few angry shouts come our way, but there's no chance for apologies now. Just ahead of us the wayward hounds are crossing the stag's line. Bolt upright on his hunter, spurring the chestnut gelding close in behind them, with the delighted yells of an escaped maniac, Tolland is urging the dogs to hunt. That's all they want to do. Yelping and howling they settle quickly to a snaking single file.

The whipper-in glances round when he hears me crashing along behind him. He looks startled to see me. As if he had thought himself alone at last and now expects me to try forcing a way past him. But I've no intention of doing that if I can help it. I'm struggling to keep this hotblood in check. But it's a battle. Kabara's fighting the curb and is not in the mood for accepting second place. For a moment it looks as though we're going to blast the whipper-in to one side and overrun his hounds!

But the going at this point settles the question for us. The aspect of the hill changes under us and we begin picking up the eerie hollow vibrations of unsound ground. Wary of this stuff, Kabara steadies at once. We wouldn't get safely through it without Tolland to pick the line for us anyway. Forced to match the pace of the dogs, he can't ease up either. Gloomy-looking stands of dark green rushes, which no doubt conceal treacherous spring-heads and bottomless black bogs, whip past us at high speed. There's a distinct tinkling, a trickling and increasingly a rushing sound of subterranean streams filling the air! Cascades beneath the surface! Unnerving at this pace. As we penetrate deeper into this quaking country we find ourselves sprinting over rotten honeycombed areas, criss-crossed with blind gutters brimming from last night's downpour. A welling-up of water on all sides. Like a monstrous rotten bag full of holes and breached seams, this great sodden spongy mountain is sucking and gurgling, noisily draining itself all around us.

I realise we must be traversing the origins of a river. Hurtling across its unsteady face I feel as though we could all be snatched into the depths of this jelly any second. A plume of black mud sprayed into the air like an exploding shell on a battlefield, then never seen again! There one minute, gone the next. Something for the guidebooks. Another unsolved Exmoor mystery for Roly-Poly and her mates to shake their heads over.

Then, as suddenly as we went into it, we're out of it. Dirty grey blobs of sheep wool hooked up here and there on briars and blackthorns that are safely rooted in rocks, there, as we come careering over the steep flank and slam straight down towards a tight sheep track, that the last hound is just disappearing into, curving its precipitous way among the stunted timber below.

There's no other way. If we want to keep those dogs in sight we've got to follow them. We dive full-throttle into this steep, shaded tunnel; the slope drops away abruptly on my left as we go in, a practically vertical wall falling hundreds of feet through the scrub and loose rocks to the white water of the torrent far below us in the bed of the dark combe. Tolland doesn't hesitate. He gallops blindly down this suicidal track, even snatching a glance back at me as he ducks in under the low branches.

Kabara's forefeet prop sharply, making him grunt with pain and sending stone-chips purring out ahead of us into the leaves of the low trees, as he plunges and skates down the scree, fighting to keep on his feet. It's a wonder his bones don't snap with the pounding. It's just a matter of clenching my teeth and hanging on to everything, hoping for the best and trying to avoid getting speared in the neck by a withered branch.

We crash out at the bottom, still on all fours and more or less in one piece. Apart from rattling stones, the track behind us is empty. We're the only ones to have followed the whip. I can't imagine the Tiger making that descent. Though I suppose he might *pick* his way down.

Turning upstream and lashing his gasping hunter along beside the foaming water without a pause, Tolland looks round at me and shouts, 'The Devil's Track!' laughing, his face flushed.

But not a second to be wasted, I'd say, or we'll be left standing here alone in the wilderness wondering where the hunt has gone. For the hounds are running mute now and we must keep them in view if we're not to lose them.

Five minutes later—we've been ducking and weaving through a plantation of larches for a good fifty yards—and I realise with a sudden shock of recognition that we're heading straight for the soiling pit of the Tivington nott. We've crossed the main stream twice and are galloping up a side-branch. There's not much time for examining the lay of the land in detail, but this is the place. I know it. I can *smell* it!

Seconds later we plunge through the great nott's pungent glade and dash in among his trees on the far side, scattering leaves and mud and twigs around us as if all this is nothing sacred! I look in to the dark shadows of the trees as we go by. Is he in there watching us? Or has he gone? Has the Haddon stag led the hunt through here today in an attempt to save himself? To rouse the nott and put the hounds on to *his* scent? To work the change and slip away, sinking his own scent down the water unseen? And has he succeeded? These people would give almost anything to catch the elusive creature that's been making a mockery of their best efforts for almost twenty years; perhaps Mrs Allen would forgive Jack Perry for accepting such a tempting change as *that*! But, a fresh deer at this advanced stage of the run would surely prove too strong for the hounds.

This Haddon stag must be almost out of straight running.

We leave the nott's secret lair behind, and the head of

the combe opens out in front of us. And there they are! Less than half a mile ahead, racing up an open zigzag path on to the grassy slope of the hill. In the clear. Making for the upland. Beyond them I see Cheyne's big grey horse bounding along in the sunlight. It's the main bunch!

Wouldn't the Tiger like to be here in my place now!

'See that!' Tolland shouts triumphantly, as if a proof of something wonderful has just been revealed, shaking his crop at them and driving his faltering horse up the slope; 'The same line he led us last autumn! He's gone out over Tarr Ball Hill!'

Tolland's delighted. Maybe he can smell success?

And as if the huntsman knew all along that we would pass this way today, as if it has not been a chase determined by the whim of the stag, the two second-horsemen he sent out earlier from the pub yard at Winsford are waiting at the top of this hill. Tolland shows no surprise to see them, but rides over to them. Perry has taken his fresh mount. His exhausted first horse, standing with head down, black with sweat, is beyond showing interest in anything. I keep going while Tolland mounts his second horse.

Kabara's blowing hard but he's got the leaders in his sights and he shakes his head and sets out after them. I'm not wearing spurs and I haven't a whip. This horse doesn't need them. I hear the horn faintly in the distance. Perry must be close to the stag. But which one? Has he viewed him? Does he know for sure what he's hunting? Or have his hounds taken the change; proved themselves false to the line and settled to the foil of the Tivington nott without him suspecting it?

Tolland sprints past us, his fresh hunter bounding and eager, as we're drawing up with the tail-end of the leaders. He gives me a wave as he dashes by. 'The Devil's Track!' he yells again, grinning like mad, and I wave back to him.

It's clear going ahead for miles. The visibility is perfect, the ground rising and falling, undulating gently to the far horizon. We're on the point of passing a rider, skirting the edge of a stand of bracken, him brushing the periphery of it, when he goes down in a spray of shredded fronds, his horse giving a hopeless grunt in mid-stride and smashing in to the earth, as if a hand had reached up and torn it off its feet. Kabara skips niftily aside, and as I look down I see his forefeet miss, by no more than an inch, a flailing sickle-end of rusty barbed wire!

But there's no stopping him! He must be picking up the wind of Harbringdon's red stud, and he's going after him, getting stronger at each stride, drawing on his deeper, more steady, reserves of strength. We're soon making our way through the field. Judging the situation. Working at it. Not charging at it blindly. Pacing it. This is the work that suits him. This is where his great spirit, his heart, his wonderful condition, and his blood will all tell. This is where—barring accidents—he will surely wear down these others, in this long open running.

Cheyne's not so far ahead of us, two hundred yards at the most. He must be cursing his error in sending his second-horseman to Winsford Hill. Even that magnificent big grey that he's riding would have to be tiring under the load, starting to struggle after being lashed and spurred and pushed to its limit all the way. I can sense Kabara's calm, his increasing confidence, feel him extending himself a little, not labouring, but pushing it that bit harder, his wind deep and sound. Settled.

A minute later we come up alongside Mrs Grant. She's going well, but I can see that her mount is tired, is staying with it, *sticking* at it despite fatigue, reaching and rolling in its stride and incapable of a better pace. She is standing up in her stirrups, leaning forward and coaxing the horse along. She'll be hoping for a check at the end of this run, hoping the stag starts going in for a few cunning ruses soon and doesn't run on without a break all the way to the Atlantic coast. Which is the way he's heading at the moment.

When she hears us coming up on her she glances round. Seeing me, she raises her eyebrows, but she doesn't say anything. We draw level and go past, spraying a few black clods her way; not that more mud is likely to worry her; her once white buckskins are filthy.

Once past Mrs Grant, apart from Perry and Tolland, there are only four riders still in front of us. A good quarter-mile in the lead, despite Cheyne's earlier hair-raising efforts, is the tall figure of Lord Harbringdon on his red stallion, bounding gracefully across the purple moor. Then comes Cheyne himself, and behind him two other riders who are unknown to me. There's no sign of Perry or his hounds, and our wayward bunch must have got up and joined them because there's no sign of them either.

Harbringdon's leading confidently almost due west along the spine of the moor. But it's not long before Tolland takes over from him—that bright pink coat again. A lure for us to chase for a while, diminishing in to the distance, then disappearing altogether into a fold in the landscape. How *he* can know the line is beyond me. He was with me until a short while ago and I saw nothing.

There must be vital clues to all this that escape me.

Before long we're looking at Cheyne's wide back. Surging up on the pounding heels of his great muscular hunter, with a hint of the Shire in its massive haunches and thighs, a war horse. And we are now close enough to see the mess of blood and rimed sweat that's flowed back and coagulated in dirty streaks, staining its grey coat from its barrel to its flanks; and to see the quivering of its belly each time Cheyne's short hunting spurs dig at the wounds. Cheyne is hard down in the saddle, an unforgiving dead weight. The grey's wind is almost spent and it's sobbing for air. We keep out a little way to the left to avoid the flying earth and twigs and the odd stone that its hooves are throwing up as it blunders across the heather.

Cheyne's so deeply intent on demanding the last ounce out of this horse that we're at his shoulder before he becomes aware of us. When he does finally see me, he glares across, looking so overheated that I half expect him to take a wild swipe at me with his crop out of sheer frustration at being overtaken. But if he has the impulse he resists it and we pass, going on and away from him. And after a few strides he shouts an afterthought at my back, ridiculing his friend the Tiger, mocking the accent; 'Hunt with him, boy!' And I hear him laughing. Or is he swearing at his horse?

I wonder if he'll be a hostile eye-witness against me for the Tiger's enquiries later?

It's hard to tell. There's no stopping now!

We're locked into this endurance run.

Kabara's stretching out his long legs and I can feel his mind set on that blood-bay stallion out there in front of us. I'm not asking anything of him, he's just doing it. I am sitting as high and as light as I can on his back, trying to float along above him, to ride so well with the rhythm of his stride that he will not have to bear my weight.

How much longer can he run like this?

I'm feeling it myself. The soft pads of skin on the insides of my knees are rubbed raw by the saddle flaps. It's these labourers' breeches! They've got sharp seams at the bend of my knees. They were not designed for hard riding. We rip across a patch of short burnt gorse, the prickles and the black points of the charred branches scratching and stabbing at Kabara's shanks. He draws breath sharply. With the pain, I sense fierceness come alight in him. Something of that insanity that I felt in him the first time I stood alongside him in Tiger's yard that day!

The saliva flicks back off his lips and the lather creams on his black neck and I begin to realise now what it is with this horse, see that I am at fault with him. While Cheyne and the Tiger and the rest of them are spurring and whipping and prodding and goading their mounts to keep them going forward, this horse will run until his heart bursts; if his rider should let him do it. The more pain he encounters the harder he goes into it. There's no *giving up* in him! A better horseman than I am would have realised this sooner! I begin talking to him, working the curb and trying to ease him down, making an effort to get through the fire that's burning in his brain. To assert a firmer authority with him. If I don't, he'll give his life to this business.

But maybe my insight has come too late.

He's off the bit. He has taken charge.

We rocket over a rise, veering sharply to our right in pursuit of the amazing and elusive Harbringdon (I'll bet *he's* in control) splashing across a wet patch; then suddenly there is the whole pack of hounds strung out in front of us. Their tongues flagging out the side of their mouths and their lips drawn back, they are wearied and muddied dogs and there are not nearly as many of them as there were when we set off. They are running for blood, silent except for the occasional whimper, pressing hard on the tail of their beaten quarry.

No more than twenty yards in front of the leading hound, reeling in his stride, head down, hard-pressed and in evident distress, making his last great effort, the Haddon stag is galloping for his life down the hill towards the dense woods and the stream. The sight of the stag makes me forget about trying to control Kabara. He is so changed that it's hard to see him as the same beast that stepped confidently out of the woods above Winsford this morning and stood in the sunlight, eyeing us calmly. Now his gait is faulty, his stride stiff and short. When he looks around, his gaze is wild and despairing, as if there isn't much more he can do. If he stumbles on this slope those big hounds will haul him to the ground. He *must* run! The steady old hounds have taken the lead. That yellow brindly one's right up there and Bellman's not more than a yard behind him.

I realise that Kabara has steadied back to a saner pace, but I don't know whether I managed to do it or whether he did it himself. And here comes Perry, cantering parallel to us up on the far hill. It looks as though he must have turned the stag back from a last attempt to get back on to the moor. And beyond him there's Mrs Allen's square, stationary car coming into view. Parked against the skyline, overlooking this combe—unmistakable with its black box on the back— ahead of us again! There's something relentless about her movements in all this. Unerring. Anticipating the line of the hunt as if she were merely *waiting* for it to happen, rather than following its course.

Harbringdon has slowed and pulled in behind the last of the hounds, cantering shoulder to shoulder with Tolland. Kabara seems content to take up a place behind them, his madness extinguished by something.

But I feel like that too.

No one is saying anything, and as the beaten stag disappears beneath the dark boughs of the larches below us, the pack roiling in behind him, a scattering of rooks rises without a sound from the upper branches of the trees and wheels away into the sky. We go in under them, the thud of our horses' hooves silenced at once by the thick layer of needles; our mounts collected, well in hand, the pace reduced to a processional lope as we descend the wide ride towards the water.

In another moment we emerge from the gloom of the plantation into a glade which leads us to the bank of a fast flowing river. A dozen or more hounds have already swum across and are clambering out a few yards downstream, where they have begun to quest for the scent of the deer; one balancing delicately on his hind legs, lifting his nose to wind an overhanging willow branch, others working out across the grass. Another bunch has headed off down the water, giving tongue and apparently close-hunting the stag; some struggle along in the water, alternately swimming and leaping from stone to stone, while the rest run along on the bank. A few of the young hounds who led the field away eagerly from Burrow Wood this morning are too overdriven to go any further and have either sat down or are standing shivering, heads drooping, tails between their legs, beyond making any further effort to work now that they have stopped; some of these may never fully recover from this murderous run.

Tolland checks the soft bank for the deer's slot, determining its direction where it entered the water. The deep fresh marks driven into the tender grass point downstream. And that's the way we go. Following the howlers! But they soon shut up, becoming uncertain of the scent, and within minutes it's clear that we've lost him!

But he can't be far away!

He's round here somewhere!

A moment of confusion, loss of direction, then Perry comes crashing down the combe through a pathless scrub ahead of us, driving stragglers in front of him and calling the staunch and seasoned hounds to him by name. Back they go, falling over each other as their master rides through them, chased by his voice and his whip, back to the point where the deer entered the water. Perry ignores us, maybe even not seeing us, and almost pushes Tolland off the bank and in to the water as he passes, working his hounds feverishly, as if he knows the stag's ruse and must unravel it within seconds or forfeit the chance forever.

We scramble out of his way, then fall in behind him. I bring up the rear after Harbringdon. We've gone only a few yards when he twists round in his saddle and points with his crop at a spot just in front of Kabara's forefeet. Looking at the spot and not at me, he says; 'Will you stand here?' and he rides on.

I suppose it's an order, so I pull up. This is my post! Watch and wait. Report enemy movements! All round us a scrubby wilderness, down to the bank and overhanging the rushing water; a tangle of thorn and willow above and an impenetrable underlayer weighted with moisture below, flood debris, dead trunks and branches, wads of leaves like banknotes.

Harbringdon and the others out of sight now.

I get off and loosen the girth. Kabara gives a big sigh and shakes himself, almost dislodging the saddle. He'd love a roll in the sand. On my feet for the first time in hours! My legs are shaky and aching. Kabara stabs at the path with his off hind hoof, so I go round and have a look. He lets me lift it. He's suffered a slicing cut to the inside of the skin just above his pastern at the base of the cannon bone. It's weeping a clear fluid on to a stain of blood around his hoof. I decide I'd better find a spot where I can get him down to the water and give it a good wash.

We're making our way along the path when he is alerted by something. He stiffens and snorts a quick breath out of his wide nostrils, gazing fixedly toward a great mat of interwoven willow fronds and rubbish, which is heaving slowly upward out of the water about ten yards in front of us. We stand and watch. Pushing up through this great sodden pad, the festooned antlers of the stag emerge. Slowly and carefully he climbs out of the pool, draped with trailing lines of weed and rubbish, garbed like a circus creature for some special performance, the water cascading from his sleeked coat. There is a blindness of fatigue about him, for he doesn't see us, sees *none* of the usual warning signs of danger, no longer sensitive to the forest about him, but searching single-mindedly for his life out of this day. I call to him softly; 'Hey, stag!' and he falters but doesn't look round. The wilderness calling his name.

I should alert the hunt, tighten my girth, leap on to Kabara's back and let rip with that cry that will bring Perry and his fierce dogs scorching down here in a hungry pack within seconds!

What then, stag? . . .

I am a hunter on station. Shall I call them?

With infinite care and daintiness he is sneaking through the tangle of scrub, his massive antlers a burden, laid back along his shoulders, his black nose pointing forward up the hill towards the moor. He is silent except for his breathing; which is a series of short, repeated sharp exhalations of breath, distinctly audible above the rushing of the water. Climbing step by step through the tangle towards the clearer going of the larch plantation, his body dark and hollowed at the flanks—he is going away!

He's giving them the slip! ·

Tolland's exultation was premature. The Haddon stag is not going out over Tarr Ball Hill this time. He has deposited no scent between the river and the path; the cascade of water would have washed it from him there. He has broken the foil! There is a gap now in the trail which a returning Perry and his dogs may pass through, going on at a loss and hunting fruitlessly down the water while their quarry returns silently to the wide moor. I watch his stealthy escape until he is out of sight up the hill and then I turn away and we go on down to the river to wash.

I'm sitting staring into the stream ten minutes later when I hear Cheyne's view halloa echoing in to the valley from the plantation above! I look at Kabara and he flexes his poll and gives my shoulder a nudge. I get up and tighten the girth. By the time we get back to the glade the stag has been hunted back in to the water, where he has gone to bay, pushing his hind quarters into the far bank and standing almost shoulder deep in the rushing stream. He is going to defend himself.

He's not like the mad bull, Vern Diplomat V11, who goes at it head down, scraping the ground with his hooves, snorting and threatening. The stag stands tense and quivering, gathered tightly into himself, upright, head held high and back, mouth firmly closed, sighting along the scalloped cheekbones of his face with his black eyes; his body arched, the stag is a drawn bow!

The hounds that are swimming at him directly are safe, as the strong current is carrying them away from him, but one bold dog has gone in above him and the current is carrying this one on to him. The stag goes back a little more, tightening his stance, drawing his sinews a final notch, his wide steady eye fixed on the approaching dog. Then suddenly he releases the tight power, lunging forward and downwards in a clean sweeping thrust that carries him eight feet or more off the bank, the white bone tip of his long brow point slipping accurately in to the paddling dog at the throat and coming out behind its right ear. The dripping carcass of the yellow brindle hound flicks out of the water and thuds in to the bank. The stag draws back again, his eye fiercer.

The other hounds moan and bay and howl their mournful howls at this, but they don't turn aside until Perry's desperate shouts threaten them with hanging, and then they draw off reluctantly, complaining and growling and giving out that deep peculiar baying sound that is sinister and needs no explanation.

Perry spurs his hunter across the river and gets behind the stag. Leaping off he quickly pieces together his gun from the various leather pouches on his saddle. Tolland, Harbringdon and Cheyne come down the ride at a gallop together, arriving in the glade as the flat crack of the gunshot cuts a pause into the howling of the dogs—in time to see the Haddon stag die, to see him collapse into the water.

Despite being on a beaten horse Cheyne is first there, jumping straight in to the river and grabbing the antlers of the stag, and showing his great strength by hauling it out on to the grass before Tolland can effectively help him.

I ride across to the far bank behind Lord Harbringdon. And we gather round. The five of us look down silently at the slack body of the dead stag where it lies at our feet on the soft green grass, and Perry blows the mort. The long shrill blasts fill the glade; the wailing lamentation of the horn cries out, echoing and re-echoing deep into the scrubby combe, and then passes back and forth and back again, rises through the dark avenues of the larches, and rises even further, winding up and out thinly at last on to the wild wide moor far above us—where the master sits in her car and waits—and finally it is lost in the wind from the Atlantic.

The hounds bay and moan, join with the huntsman, prowling and skulking and slinking around behind us, their patience worn thin, clamouring for their reward. And so Perry stuffs the horn in to his jacket finally and takes out his hunting knife. We move back a pace as he lays the stag on its back and slits it up the belly. The guts and lungs and all the rest of the steaming contents hang out on to the grass, still attached at the windpipe; till Perry severs it and it falls free in a gurgling mass. He retrieves the liver from this stinking pile and he and Tolland drag the rest of the carcass away a few yards, before giving the hounds their signal.

In go the dogs with a rush, growling, ravenous, frenzied for a full share, spraying shit and blood and bits of torn white membrane around. They've finished the lot in less than a minute, rolling and scuffling and sneezing and shaking themselves and licking their dirtied muzzles with rapture.

The staghounds' party.

There's a pause. Perry is standing holding the knife, dangling in his hand, his other hand holding the top point of the stag's antlers, waiting to go on with his work. He and Tolland exchange a look and Tolland reaches into the cavity of the stag's carcass. He comes up with a handful of blood, holding his dripping palm away from his body in front of him. We watch him. Waiting to see what he will do. He takes two quick strides towards me and splashes the blood in my face.

They all look at me and say nothing as I recoil and try to wipe the wretched stuff off. I see Harry Cheyne's hard features, his gaze focused on me, and Lord Harbringdon's pale grey eyes, remote and slightly hooded, turned for this instant in my direction, including me in the group. And in front of me Tolland, his open and generous features for this occasion unsmiling.

'Fair hunting, boy,' he says, and Perry and the other two voice their ready agreement.

Perry bends to his task and severs the stag's head.

I ride away from the death alone, and it comes to me at once that it is the ambivalence in the heart of the Tiger that keeps him from their company at the kill, not the lack of a good horse. His passion for the hunt is not complete enough for him to risk everything as Tolland and the others do. The Tiger takes his scheming with him wherever he goes.

I encounter Mrs Grant making her way down the combe to the kill, leading her beaten horse. She pauses and I stop on the path and look down at her.

'Was it the right deer?' she asks.

'Yes.'

I meet no one else. The moor paths are deserted. I think about Mrs Grant's question and wonder if I really saw the Tivington nott today, standing like a prehistoric stone among the larches, watching the hunt go by; or whether I just wish that I had seen him. I look around me at the wide deserted sweep of the moor and I feel sure that that strange creature is its only inhabitant besides myself. The hundreds of riders who began the day with us are gone. It is as if there has been no hunting. I finger the coarse hairs of the blood-stained slot given me by Perry at the last moment; shoving it into my hand without a word. I have it in the side pocket of my jacket.

When we reach the heights of Heydon Hill the valley is laid out below us all the way to the coast. Kabara halts. The sun is low in the sky at our backs, hanging huge and red over the grey Atlantic, and the shadow of the hill is cast far across the lowlands before us; fields, roads, villages, towns, smoke rising and tiny cars threading their way.

I am reluctant to go down. I believe I shall never come up here again. I stroke Kabara's neck and he snorts and shakes his head, as if he understands what I have done for him. Lord Harbringdon was delighted to hear from me that this great horse is for sale; he is certain tomorrow to offer Alsop a price for Kabara which the Tiger will not be able to match. The Tiger is already well enough mounted. I shall tell him. I shan't make a secret of what I've done. I'll let him know he's lost. Roly-Poly was right all the time; her farm is not a fit place for me or for Kabara. Kabara has found *his* place.

We look for a moment longer in to the darkening valley. Across the other side are the Quantock Hills, their contours softened by the last pale sunlight; and lying between, what Morris calls the valley without a name. I nudge Kabara in the flank and he moves off, beginning the long descent. I have begun to think of the many good things I am about to lose. For Kabara's sake I regret nothing, but I wonder what it is that I am making my own way towards.

Prochownik's Dream
Alex Miller

Toni Powlett is an artist in the grip of a crisis. Since the death of his father, Moniek Prochownik, four years earlier, Toni has been at a creative standstill—until Marina Golding, the wife of his former teacher and mentor, Robert Schwartz, contacts him, and everything changes. Toni finds in Marina the perfect companion of his life in art and his creative energies are re-awakened.

But Toni's newfound inspiration and artistic energy come at the direct expense of his relationship with his wife and daughter. The more dependent for his art he becomes on Marina, the more potentially destructive become the tensions between himself and his wife, Teresa. Toni's dilemma is how to reconcile the transgressive nature of his imaginative life with the daily life of his family, who he loves. Robert Schwartz's dying father, Theo, warns him not to confuse art with life. But by what means is he to achieve such clear-sightedness?

Immensely satisfying, *Prochownik's Dream* is a work of great subtlety, strength and intellect. Its examination of the artist at work is complex and completely absorbing. But at its heart, very simply, it is a book about love.

ISBN 1 74114 249 0

Journey to the Stone Country
Alex Miller

WINNER OF THE MILES FRANKLIN LITERARY AWARD

Betrayed by her husband, Annabelle Beck retreats from Melbourne to her old family home in tropical North Queensland where she meets Bo Rennie, one of the Jangga tribe. Intrigued by Bo's claim that he holds the key to her future, Annabelle sets out with him on a path of recovery that leads back to her childhood and into the Jangga's ancient heartland, where their grandparents' lives begin to yield secrets that will challenge the possibility of their happiness together.

With the consummate artistry of a novelist working at the height of his powers, Miller convinces us that the stone country is not only a remote and exotic location in North Queensland, but is also an unvisited place within each of us. *Journey to the Stone Country* confirms Miller's reputation as one of Australia's most intelligent and uncompromising writers.

'The most impressive and satisfying novel of recent years. It gave me all the kinds of pleasure a reader can hope for.'
—Tim Winton

ISBN 1 74114 146 X